Books by Dan Gerber

POETRY

The Revenant
Departure
The Chinese Poems
Snow on the Backs of Animals
A Last Bridge Home: New and Selected Poems
Trying to Catch the Horses

NOVELS

American Atlas
Out of Control
A Voice from the River

SHORT STORIES

Grass Fires

NONFICTION

Indy: The World's Fastest Carnival Ride

Grass Fires

GRASS FIRES

STORIES BY

DAN GERBER

For Emily Pease,
with my best wishes for
your work,
Dan Gerber
October

CLARK CITY PRESS

Clark City Press
Post Office Box 1358
Livingston, Montana 59047

For Judith, Patricia and Robert

Bovary is me.

FLAUBERT

CONTENTS

Yard Sale 1

The Way A Woman Thinks 9

Home 19

Crop Duster 27

A Dapper Little Man 36

One Morning In May 43

Lorraine 60

Conversation 68

Grass Fires 77

Hardball 84

New People 91

Sharon 102

Elinor 109

Roy 117

Things Are Closer Than They Appear 124

Small Talk 129

Shelter 139

Suspicion 147

The Night Is Growing Longer 154

Homecoming 165

Grass Fires

YARD SALE

I don't think there's anything prettier than west Michigan this time of May. Dogwood, lilacs, apple blossoms against the undarkened green of new leaves and new grass. I thought about that driving in to work this morning. Alice was having a yard sale, and I had Saturday E.R. duty. I don't like yard sales. They've always seemed to me like airing your dirty laundry. All the cast-off debris of people's lives laid out on tables to be picked over by anyone who's curious. I never liked going to them, and I argued against having this one, but Alice runs the house and has her way. She says it's just because I'm a Pisces. I'll put empty toothpaste tubes back in the medicine cabinet, and she'll go through and clean them out, replace my worn-out toothbrushes and restock. I can't argue with her. But to see all those old things put together on display—bicycles, roller skates, Ray Jr.'s baseball shoes—a picture of what we aren't anymore. I worried about Alice's handling the empty nest, the kids grown and gone, but I guess I'm the one.

Jill's married and works for IBM in Cincinnati, and Ray Jr.'s in his third year of law school. I'm proud of them both, but sometimes I don't know what I'm doing anymore. I've been a doctor almost thirty years now, and it isn't what I thought it would be. I had some idea about being the country doctor when I came here from Detroit. A kind of missionary. I'm not religious, I don't mean that, but they were desperate here, and I chose it over catching babies in Bloomfield Hills. I would bring good medicine to the sticks. But this isn't the sticks. It's a place, a good place, and when I go back to Detroit, that's what seems strange to me.

But it's never gotten any easier to tell someone they're dying or to tell their husband or their wife or their children. I thought I'd grow into these things. But how do you tell a man that his daughter you've treated all her life has died of something people just don't die of? It was like some kind of tasteless joke. I did everything that was indicated, but she didn't respond. I gave her oxygen and an I.V. to rehydrate her. I put her on aminophylline and adrenalin, an I.P.P.B. I intubated her, and nothing worked.

She was a friend of my daughter's when they were in school. She spent weekends at our house, and she and Jill would put on plays in the basement and charge us a quarter admission. She would giggle before every line and then pull herself in and deliver it beautifully and then giggle again at the very idea that she had actually said something like, "Oh Oswald, you are the source of all my woe."

I remember that because it was the last line she said before the power went out. It had been thundering outside and they finished the play by candlelight. Ray Jr., who was younger than the girls, played all the bit parts. "Now I'm the raven; now I'm the messenger; now I'm the tall pine tree," they would have him say. Jill directed and kept the show going. "Now be serious," she would say. But when she got past her giggles, Nancy was what kept our interest. She said her lines like she believed them, and she made us believe them too. She brought me close to tears a couple of times. They were silly little plays the kids had made up, but sometimes Nancy would take off with a speech that hadn't been planned. She'd see something or feel something and talk about the ring of trees where she was to meet her prince, how she would go there every night till the end of time, even though he never returned from the Crusades. Nancy could have read the telephone book and made us cry.

Jill went off to college, and Nancy got married right out of high school. We predicted it wouldn't work, and it didn't. She had a baby, a little girl, and six months later her husband went to California. He got work with a company that built greenhouses. He sent money back, child support, and a year after that, he married again.

And today Nancy died in the emergency room. I'd read of patients dying of asthma attacks. I'd read of people dying of measles, but you don't expect to see it in a small town E.R. You expect cardiacs and farm and highway accidents, drownings in the summer, gunshot wounds in the fall. But you don't expect a beautiful young woman with a six-year-old daughter to suffocate in your arms on what might have been the prettiest day of the year. I felt betrayed. I felt Nancy had done this to me, that she was being dramatic, that she had made it all up. She was crying and pleading with me not to let her die. "My little girl," she gasped out in that horrible wheezing voice, those faint words squeezed out from the back of the throat. "Nancy, you're okay," I said. I stroked her hair. "Relax and your breath will come back." I knew I could save her. I'd been through this same kind of thing a hundred times before. But she didn't relax, and her breath didn't come back, and I went into a rage. "Nancy, God damn it! Don't do this!" I pounded the gurney with my fist. I shook her. I cried. I threw my stethoscope across the room. The nurses and orderlies were embarrassed for me. They shrank back out of the way as if they thought I might hit someone. I walked to the doctors' lounge, and I closed the door. I couldn't talk to Bob Russell. If she'd been in a car crash and bled to death, I could have handled it. I could've said, "We did everything we could."

YESTERDAY WHEN I WAS HELPING Alice get ready for her yard sale, she brought something down from the attic, something I didn't know we even owned, something I didn't want to see. It was a hassock, flat on top and sewn in triangles of leather on the sides so that it resembled a snare drum. It had been my father's footstool in our house in Ferndale when I was a child. It must be the same one. I can't imagine we would've found another one like it, or if we had, that I would have let Alice buy it. I don't know how it could have ended up in our attic. It was the stool that had sat in front of my father's Morris chair. My father would come home from work at G.M. and plop down in the chair and put his feet on that hassock, and that's where he lived. My memories of my father are almost exclusively memories of him sitting in that chair. Sometimes when he was at work and I'd come home from school, I'd look at the chair and see how his body had broken it down to a mold, a negative image. Several times I tried the chair, but it just wasn't comfortable. I would get up right away with a feeling I'd done something wrong.

But the hassock held its shape. For all the years his feet rested on it, it stayed flat on top. Maybe he hadn't had it as long as he'd had the chair. I don't know. He and my mother had been married ten years before I came along, and the chair and the hassock were there.

My father died in that chair. I found him in it one spring morning when I got up to read the Sunday comics. He'd been working on our travel-trailer in the driveway a few days earlier, when it slipped on the jacks and an axle bumped his head. He seemed to be all right at first, but something had changed. He looked funny, and he was quiet. I was only ten, and I thought he was angry. On that Saturday morning he hit my sister because she had been late getting home from a date Friday night. I'd never seen a grown-up hit anyone before. Neither he nor my mother had ever hit me. Mother stepped in and stopped it. She told us to stay away from him. She said he was sick, and that's why he looked at us the way he did.

Then that Sunday morning I came downstairs. I got the funny papers from the porch and took them to the living room. At first I thought he was sleeping, that he'd fallen asleep in his chair. But then I saw the blood on his face and his .22 Colt Woodsman on the floor beside him. I don't know why no one had heard the shot. He was sitting there with his eyes open and his head slumped down so that it seemed as if he were looking at the hassock. And then I looked at the hassock and saw that there were three bullets on it, all standing on end in a row. I'll never know, of course, but I thought right then of my sister, my mother and me.

After the funeral, my mother had some men come and get the chair. I don't know what they did with it, but I pushed the hassock back into the corner of the room and covered it with the drapes by the French doors that opened out to the back yard, and I don't remember ever seeing it again until Alice brought it down from the attic.

I THOUGHT ABOUT THE HASSOCK as I sat there in the doctors' lounge, thought of it emerging again now and wondered about all those years between. I thought of the yard sale going on at that moment, of the past being sold off, the bicycles finding new riders, the roller skates new sidewalks, the props and costumes of our basement theater finding new homes, new stories; not people finding things, but things finding new lives. I thought about the things Nancy had used in her life, the English saddle she'd been so proud of, the rag doll called Luka she brought with her when she would come to spend the night.

I heard the nurse calling my name, "Dr. Walsh. Dr. Walsh," but I didn't respond till she put her hand on my shoulder. "Dr. Walsh. Mr. Russell. He's waiting."

I'd never known Bob Russell well. We'd passed a few words years before when he would bring Nancy in to our house to visit Jill or when I would drop Jill off for a weekend on their farm. He was a quiet man, not taciturn as farmers often are, as if they knew something they weren't going to tell you. Bob Russell was just a little bit shy. I found him in the lobby, sitting quietly, looking at his hands, as if in church, waiting for the service to begin. He stood up when he saw me, and he held out his hand. I wanted to say something original. I wanted to talk about the beautiful weather, some way of telling him that wouldn't be painful. It's tough enough just losing a patient. "Bob, I'm sorry," I said. "We did everything we could."

ON THE WAY HOME, I wondered why it couldn't have been raining. It was that one day when the apple trees and flowering crabs are in perfect bloom, and you know it can't last.

I didn't tell Alice about Nancy. I will in time. I'll have to call Jill and tell her. The bicycles had sold, the roller skates, the half-scale electric Model "A" I'd bought the kids on Jill's twelfth birthday, even Ray Jr.'s baseball shoes. Alice was pleased. Way more than half the stuff she had laid out was gone. But nobody bought the hassock.

"Carrie DeFrees looked at that," Alice told me. "She put it with the rest of her stuff, and then she brought it back. 'Too colonial,' she said."

"I'd kind of hoped this one would go," I said.

"You can take it to the dump if you want to," Alice sighed. She was totaling up her sales on a clipboard. It was the end of a hot afternoon, and I was tired. I sat down on the hassock and looked at the few things that were left: a box of odd buttons, an assortment of cookie cutters, an upright hair dryer, the old push lawn mower I'd used on my parents' yard in Ferndale.

After dinner I helped Alice clean up the yard. I wheeled the lawn mower back to its corner in the toolshed and felt nostalgic about the clatter it made. We folded up the tables and stored them along the wall of the garage, and I carried the hassock back up to the attic. We took a walk around the neighborhood before it got dark.

"It feels like summer," Alice said. "You should get out your video camera and get these blossoms on tape. One good rain and they'll all be gone."

"I will," I said. "I'll do it tomorrow."

THE WAY

A WOMAN THINKS

I love to watch Norman work out on a fly. It's like a ballet or something, the way the white line loops out against the dark trees. Like rope tricks or a magic show. I don't know how he does it, but I probably catch more fish than he does, with only a worm on. Sometimes I'll put on a Mepps or something and cast, but then maybe the line gets all screwed up on the reel. Norman says it's 'cause girls' elbows are built funny, but I don't think it matters. He says catching fish is nice, but that's not the point. "Gracie," he'll say, "if all I wanted was fish, I'd use a net."

Norman's my brother, but he could be my father. He's old enough. He'd been living in New York for three years when our parents died. And until he moved back to look after me, he was mostly just someone my mother cried over and my father wouldn't talk about. He was married once too, to somebody named Kate, but I never met her. He said he wouldn't have come back if it wasn't for me, but that now he was glad that he had. He says home's the best place for a writer. And he says that the best thing our Mom and Dad ever did was make me.

Norman doesn't always keep the fish he catches, either. He takes 'em off the hook and kisses 'em, actually goes smack on their lips and then throws 'em back. He says he does it 'cause they've brought him pleasure, but I think it's because he doesn't want to clean them. Norman always finds a way to get out of cleaning fish. I don't mind, even though it's yucky to pull the guts out. I love a mess of perch or blue gills fried up with butter and flour. Norman's as good a cook as anybody.

I like being alone with Norman, just us on the river or the lake with the sound of the water and the birds. There are always birds to watch. I like kingfishers the best. They look like some punker with greasy hair, and they swoop down over the water, and chatter away like idiots, like they own everything. Once I saw an osprey come out of the woods with a snake in its claws and circle the sun three times, like something out of a fairy tale. That was on the Muskegon. Norman says you can see all kinds of things when you're fishing that you can't see otherwise, because when you're fishing you're not really there in the ordinary sense, not just collecting sights, but really a part of things that are happening. He said that the animals don't see you as a person anymore. They see you as a crane or a heron or any other thing like that. He said that once at a place called Hellroaring Creek, he saw an eagle swoop down and pounce on a rabbit and tear its heart out and eat it while the rabbit still kicked at the eagle's breast feathers, like it was trying to push it away. When he told me about it, his eyes got like there was some important message I was supposed to get out of it, but I just mostly thought it was gross.

Norman says I'm probably his best fishing companion. He says being with me's almost as good as being alone because I don't have to talk all the time. He gets plenty of talk with Bonita. I lie awake in the dark and listen to them in the kitchen, talking. They fight a lot, and I think it's because Bonita's too smart for her own good. Norman's the smartest person I know, and he's famous. You see his books everywhere. He's been on TV, and they write about his books in the magazines. I've been to New York with Norman, three times. We went to the Empire State Building and lots of museums and Radio City, and I got to sit in the studio and watch when he went on the "Today" show. I wish Mom and Dad could've known how famous Norman was gonna be. I remember Dad used to say Norman was a useless bum and a troublemaker. I think I remember, or maybe Norman told me that. I was only nine when their car went off the bridge.

I asked Norman why he never writes about fishing, and he said that when he writes he's somewhere else, some other time and place and that fishing is how he gets back into the world. Norman's not like other guys in Brainard, but he tries to be. When we go down to the Co-op to buy feed for the goat, he hangs around and talks about how we need rain and what the price of corn might be in the fall and stuff he thinks will make him sound like a farmer. It makes me laugh. "Why do you do that, Norman?" I ask him. "You don't know beans about farming."

"Ink for the pen," he says. "I have to know how real people talk."

"Real people?"

I wish I was a boy. I know it'd be easier if I was. Then Norman could talk to me about all the things men talk about. When he's drinking, he talks about women like they were skunks or some other kind of animal you wouldn't want around. He says he doesn't mean me, says I'm different, but still . . . I don't want to grow up to be a bitch. Norman says Bonita's a bitch. She's from the Philippines; that's what she says anyway, and she's real dark and beautiful. They argue, and they drink a lot, and they laugh. Sometimes I hear them laughing through the wall of my room. Bonita's laugh is low and husky, like someone with a cold. And then they're quiet, and then I hear the bed squeaking and the headboard banging against the wall and Bonita laughing again.

There is something about Bonita though, something that draws Norman to her, the way insects gather on the screens on summer nights when the lights are on in the house. And maybe it's the same things that makes him hate her sometimes. Once when Bonita and I were driving home from Bill's Shop 'n Save, she said, "You're lucky, you know it, Gracie? You've got the best part of Norman without his meanness. I wish Norman could be friends with me like he is with you."

"Did you and Norman have a fight?" I asked her.

"We always fight, honey," she said.

I felt funny when she called me that, but I liked it too. I like Bonita the best of any of the women Norman's had around, better than Beverly or Lois, and I wish I could let her be friends with me. But I know it wouldn't last.

"I'm sorry Bonita," I said, "that you and Norman fight, I mean." She reached over and squeezed my hand, and I could see that she was about to cry, and we didn't say anything else all the way home.

Sometimes, when Bonita says something funny, Norman claps his hands and kisses her and says she's brilliant, about like

the way he carries on when I get all A's on my report card. And
sometimes he yells, "You bitch, you stupid slut," and they
throw things at each other and pull hair and scream. And in the
morning Bonita's gone and Norman's sick from drinking too
much Jack Daniels. I find him asleep in the kitchen when I'm
getting ready for school, slumped over the table with his face
in a puddle of his own drool. I'm glad we live in the country.
I don't know what'd happen if we had neighbors. One time I
came home from school and Norman had shot holes in the wall
so you could see the sun coming through. He was sitting at the
kitchen table with his .22 Remington across his lap, and he said
he was trying to see how close he could come to the "3" on the
wall clock without really hitting it.

But don't think Norman's not a good person for me to live
with. He helps me with my homework, except for math. He's
no good at math and says so like he wouldn't want to be good at
it even if he could. And he takes me fishing about any time I
want to go. That's one thing he doesn't do with Bonita or any
other woman I know of. "You only go fishing with someone
you really like," he says.

"Don't you like Bonita?" I ask.

"I love Bonita," he says. He strokes his mustache and sucks
on the ends of it where it comes to the corners of his mouth.
"Sometimes I need Bonita." He gets up from the table where
he's been helping me diagram sentences, and he goes over to
the counter and pours some whiskey into a juice glass. "But I
don't like Bonita. She's not a friend of mine. She's not someone
you'd like to go fishing with."

Bonita takes me shopping with her sometimes in Muskegon,

13

and once she took me to a symphony concert in Grand Rapids 'cause she had tickets and Norman didn't want to go. I thought it was nice of her, even if the music was kind of slow and predictable, but Norman said she just did it to make him think she'd be a good mother for me. He says no woman who tries so hard to be a good mother could ever be one. I don't understand that. It seems to me everybody's got to try or they'll never be anything. Sometimes when Norman gets off on one of his screwy ideas about people, I just leave him alone. I figure it's 'cause he's a writer. Some of the writers who've come to visit have been pretty strange. One of 'em wouldn't eat anything but brown rice and egg whites, and he got up at the crack of dawn every morning and burned incense and chanted a lot of *Om* stuff on the front porch. Then one night he ate some roast beef Norman had cooked and drank almost a whole bottle of brandy, all by himself. And when he got sick, he said it was because Norman served him meat, even though Norman knew he was a vegetarian. Norman took him fishing and said the guy talked all the time about how unfair the critics had been about his last book, and then he got careless climbing out of the river and broke the tip of the Orvis bamboo rod Norman had loaned him. And the next time Norman and I went fishing, he took that guy's book and tore it up, page by page, and threw it in the Au Sable River.

"WILL WE ALWAYS BE FRIENDS, Norman?" I ask him. I put down my *Warriner's Grammar* and rest my chin in my hands.

The whiskey beads on his mustache hairs, and he sucks at it

with his lower lip. "Oh yes, Gracie, we'll always be friends." He takes another sip of the whiskey and leans across the table and looks me real close in the eye like he wants me to be sure he's telling the truth. "And do you know why we'll always be friends?" His voice is real soft and low so I have to listen very carefully to hear what he's saying.

"Why?" I almost have to keep from laughing, he looks so serious.

"Because we'll never be lovers, that's why. Because you're what I'd be if just one little Y chromosome had got switched around in a fit of passion thirty-five years ago. You remember when we studied about what makes people men and women?"

"Yes." I almost whisper, 'cause I never know what's gonna happen next when he gets that look on his face.

"Well you are my good and true friend," he says, "and you're too intelligent to argue with, and, most of all, you don't think like a woman."

"How does a woman think?" I ask that 'cause I want to know how not to be. I don't want the way a woman thinks to sneak up on me the way menstruation did. When menstruation came I didn't want Norman to know, and I put toilet paper in my pants and hid or burned my underpants all that week whenever they got bloody. I just wanted being a woman to go away because I thought it would wreck things between Norman and me. But then Norman found a pair of my panties under the cot on the porch, and he said, "What's this?" And he told me I couldn't just pretend I was a little girl anymore, and he told me to buy some Kotex, and the next day he took me perch fishing over on the White Lake Channel at Lake Michigan like we used to do when I was little and which is still my favorite kind of fishing.

"Don't you worry about how a woman thinks," Norman said, "because you won't think like one, not with me anyway. A woman thinks about what she can get from a man the way a bear thinks about getting honey from a tree. She sees the right kind of man, and all she sees is a big glob of honey, and the little windows in her brain start opening and snapping shut. She may not even know it. It just comes over her the way some butterflies migrate to Mexico without even knowing why."

Norman is always saying things like that, things that sound real vivid but that don't necessarily make any sense unless you push him on it. And if you do, he makes up another story to make you believe the first one was true. I remember one time when I was little and I'd had a bad dream about being chased by huge snakes in the woods, and Norman came into my room in the middle of the night and picked me up and held me in his arms and told me I was never to be afraid of anything. "Not even if evil sucks the windows out of your house. Don't be afraid," he said.

Evil sucks the windows out of your house? I could just see evil out there in the dark, sucking on the windows. But what did he mean? I asked him. "How could anything suck the windows out of a house?"

"Oh Jesus, Gracie, believe me. It's like . . . it's like . . ." And then it was like a light bulb went on over his head, like when someone gets an idea in the cartoons, and he says, "But no, I'll tell you. A tornado, that's how." And he laughed like he'd just won at Trivial Pursuit or something. "A tornado comes by and sucks all the pressure out of the air around the house, and then there's so much pressure left inside that the windows blow out like it was full of dynamite."

But I was still afraid of thinking like a woman. I wasn't afraid of menstruation anymore, but it came every month anyway, and I was afraid that before I knew it, I'd be after what I could get out of Norman, and we wouldn't be friends anymore, and I'd be a lonely conniving bitch like Bonita or Beverly or Lois, the one before her.

IT WAS MID-JULY, and the perch would be running. I put a minnow on my hook and let the sinker carry it down till I felt it tunk on the bottom. Then I cranked it up about four turns on the reel and imagined it there, just off the sand, where a yellow perch coming in from the big lake would see it just waiting there for him, like a piece of candy or a take-out order from McDonald's, or a big glob of honey. I don't think Norman will ever get married again. There'll be other Bonitas and Beverlies, but he won't really like them for very long. I guess we'll go on sharing the house with Bonita till Norman trades her in on a new one.

We sat there for a long time, maybe half an hour, but the perch weren't biting. We watched boats full of salmon fishermen with downriggers idling out the channel to Lake Michigan. Some had so many rods sticking up they looked like porcupines. Norman drank a couple of beers, and I skimmed a few dead minnows out of the bucket and tossed 'em to the seagulls

17

that were hanging around overhead. It was so quiet a big yellow butterfly came and landed on my rod. She sat there for a couple of minutes, and then she took off again. I watched her wobble out over the lake. Maybe she was headed toward Mexico, I thought, and I wondered how she'd ever make it all the way across.

HOME

It had been twenty years since we moved to town, since I took an accounting job with Clark's, and Karen and I rented the upstairs of a house on Maple Street, which we later bought. All those years, Mother lived alone on the family farm with a series of dogs and goats and finally with a parakeet named Schnapps. It seemed that all her life had been given over to being somebody's mother, and then she became everybody's child. The hard part of it was that she remained so physically able. It wasn't as if she were withering away, but the woman everyone had looked to for so many years wasn't there.

"Mother is cold," she said one afternoon when I had stopped over to help her get her papers in order before tax time. It was a raw March afternoon, intermittent rain with traces of snow, and a hard east wind growled at the windows. "Mother is upstairs, and she needs more clothes."

At first I thought she was kidding, that maybe this was some old farm way of talking about the weather, like, "The old man is snoring," something I'd forgotten or ignored in my childhood. We were going over receipts of major purchases she'd made during the year to make sure we took full advantage of the sales tax deduction.

"Now these are from the lumberyard." She handed me the slips. "Shingles, tarpaper, and new flooring for the porch. I had 'em bill me direct like you said I should, and I kept that separate from Parker's labor."

"Good," I said. "That makes it easy. Now hardware. Do you have any bills for hardware, nails, flashing, any other materials he used?"

"Yes," she said, and turned back to her folder. We were sitting at the old table in the kitchen, the kitchen that had hardly changed since my earliest memories. She had replaced the woodstove with a gas range about a year after Dad died. He had been struck by lightning, trying to finish the plowing before the rain came. I must've been about six at the time. I remember wandering in from the living room and thinking how strange it was to see Dad lying there on the table. Mother'll be mad, I thought. I remember her hollering at Nick once when he just sat on the table while he was talking to her and she was rolling out pie dough. I just had one glimpse of Dad, his head lolled back with his mouth open and one arm hanging down as if reaching to dab some spot with his finger on the blue linoleum floor. Just that one glimpse before my sister, Marlis, took me by the shoulders, turned me around and pulled me back on the couch. "Daddy's okay," she said. "He's hurt bad, but he'll be okay." And then Mother started sobbing, pulling everything in like she was choking or hiccupping or swallowing her tongue. That's what I remember about that day. And I remember the rain and the thunder that had killed him still rumbling.

Mother sorted through the file, licking her finger several

times to catch the corners of the pages. The wind picked up while she was looking for the bills for the hardware. A groan rose through the eaves like a chorus of voices, and that was when she said it. She looked across the table at me, with her finger still in the file, and asked me to take some clothes to her mother upstairs. "Please do it now," she said, and I realized she was serious. "She's freezing."

I got up from the table, walked into the living room, up the stairs and into her bedroom. I looked at the hand-tinted photographs of Marlis, Nick, Lyle and me as children, hanging on the wall by the long oval mirror, and at the worn copy of *Lady Chatterley's Lover* on the dresser, and I smiled, remembering how she had forbidden me to read it when I was in high school, "because it's a beautiful book," she had said, "and I'm afraid you'll just think it's funny." I looked at the wedding photo of her and Dad in front of the Aetna Chapel and thought about how skinny they both looked. Then I turned around and came back downstairs. I walked back into the kitchen and took my seat. "She's fine," I said.

"Thank you," she said, very politely. "Here's the hardware receipts," she said, and handed them to me across the table as if nothing had interrupted us.

That was the first time her mother intruded, the first indication that anything was going wrong, and I was as amazed at how naturally I had played along with her request and how easily the incident had passed as I was by the fact that it had happened in the first place. We finished her tax work, and she asked if I'd care to stay for dinner. I would've, I suppose, if I hadn't had a school board meeting that evening. Driving home, I thought of how there'd been times my mind had wandered off from what I was doing, how I'd called people by the wrong names, people I knew perfectly well. I thought about how she wasn't getting any younger. I figured she'd be eighty-three in May. Things like that'll happen, I told myself. Still, she was a pretty remarkable woman. She looked after the house, did the laundry, cooked for herself and sometimes would have Nick or Lyle or Karen and me over for dinner. And last summer when Marlis had come back visiting from Los Angeles with her boyfriend, Max, the film producer, Mother had joked about how they were "doubled up in Marlis's old room, saving space." I thought again about how I had gone upstairs to check on her mother. "Weird," I said to myself and shrugged my shoulders and laughed about it as I drove toward town. I didn't even think to mention it to Karen.

I spoke with Mother once over the weekend, answered her questions about what did and what did not qualify as charitable deductions. Her contributions to the President's reelection fund, for example, were among those that didn't qualify. "Ronald knows me," she said, before we said good-bye.

"Ronald?"

"The president, dear. Ronald Reagan." There was a slight edge of condescension in her voice, as if she might have added, "Stupid!" after she'd hung up, and I remembered a birthday greeting she had received from the White House last year, the kind they send to regular contributors.

IT WAS ON A TUESDAY morning at 3:13 when she called again. Out of habit, I noted the glowing numerals of the digital clock in the dark of the bedroom and felt that prickly sensation over my face that accompanies the anticipation of an emergency: our son, away at college, involved in an accident or our daughter calling to tell us she'd eloped. I didn't recognize her voice at first.

"Is your mother there?" she said.

"What?"

"Your mother. Is she there?"

My mother isn't a jokester, but she's not beyond mischief. "No, she's not," I said, not absolutely certain I wasn't dreaming.

"Oh. Well when do you expect she'll be home?"

"But you *are* my mother," I said.

"No. I'm Clara Murphy." She sounded a bit indignant, and I remembered having fallen into a well pit when I was a child, how I had tried to climb the steep walls and how the dirt kept crumbling away in my hands, and I thought I would die until Nick came and laughed and lowered down a rope.

"Yes, you are Clara Murphy," I said, "and I'm Theron Murphy, and you're my mother."

"I don't get it," she said. "Your mother isn't home?"

"No, she's not," I said. I remembered the episode about the clothes for her mother and how quickly it had passed. "Could I have her call you when she comes in?"

"No. Just tell her to stay home," she said with disgust, and then she hung up.

I couldn't get back to sleep.

"What was that all about?" Karen asked, and I told her what had been said and explained what had happened that afternoon a week earlier.

"It happens." She rolled back over on her side and gathered in her pillow with her arm. "I'm just glad it wasn't the children," she sighed.

IN THE WEEK THAT FOLLOWED there were more calls, one from a woman who identified herself as Verna Wilson, and who said that Mother had called her three times on three separate nights to tell her that she needed help, that her mother wasn't being cared for and she couldn't manage it alone.

"She's your grandmother," Mrs. Wilson insisted. "You can't put the whole burden on your mother. She's your responsibility."

As far as I knew, my grandmother had died when my mother was a child, died of pneumonia in the wagon coming out here from Pennsylvania. That seems strange to contemplate today, but that's how they came to Michigan in 1912. Mother had looked after her own father until he died in 1935, and Marlis told me that Mother had been like a mother to him, as far back as she remembered, and that he had never been quite all there after my grandmother died.

So that's how it was. I began spending more time looking after my imaginary grandmother to placate my mother's concerns for her. I took her mother to the doctor, drove to town and came back a few hours later and told her the doctor had said Grandma was fine. I even bought a new dress for Grandma, a blue dress for Easter. I didn't know about the size, but it was "just perfect," Mother said.

Nick and Lyle had a few similar adventures. I had explained what had happened, and they played along. Marlis said she could get time off and would come out if we needed her, but I didn't see any point in it. We talked about putting her in the county retirement home but agreed she was physically just too able and wouldn't stay there. We hired a nurse to live with her, but after a week, Mother fired her. She said the nurse had been rude to her mother and that her Mother had told her she didn't want anyone but her to care for her. I didn't know what to do, or if there was anything that could be done. She stopped going out, and Nick and Lyle and our wives did the shopping for her on alternate weeks.

Then one evening I stopped by after work. I had called her that noon to tell her I'd be by and to see if there was anything she might need from the store. She was sitting at the kitchen table when I got there. She had her coat on and a Sunday felt hat with a veil, something I hadn't seen her wear since I was a child. There were four large suitcases on the floor at her side, and she told me she and her mother wanted to go home.

"We've had enough of this place," she sighed. "They never cook enough food for us. Would you take us home right now, please?"

That's how she went to the county home. I carried her suit-cases while she walked her imaginary mother out and helped her into the car. Carl Banks, the administrator at the home, was an old friend from 4-H, and I got him aside and explained the situation. He said it was unusual, but that if we could pay the fees, they could take her in. He did caution me, however, that since she was so physically able they couldn't be ultimately responsible if she should wander away, and I agreed to sign a paper to that effect.

MOTHER'S QUITE HAPPY there now. They put her in with Mrs. Whiteman, who stares into space all day, and Mother looks after her. She calls Mrs. Whiteman "Mother," and Mrs. Whiteman doesn't seem to mind. I even saw her smile at Mother once after Mother had fluffed up Mrs. Whiteman's pillows, and the nurse who was in the room at the time said it was the first expression Mrs. Whiteman had shown in the three years she had been in the home.

When I go to visit her now, I take flowers for Mrs. Whiteman. In Mother's mind, Mrs. Whiteman has become my mother, too. "Your mother's been so good this week," she said, beaming with pleasure over her charge. "She ate almost all of her oatmeal, and we had a nice ride in the chair down to D wing, didn't we, dear."

I told Mother how much we all appreciated the fine work she was doing.

"No trouble at all," she said, "it's my job," and she wheeled Mrs. Whiteman off down the hall.

CROP DUSTER

Maybe it was the chemicals. I don't know. They've got all kinds of warnings about what the stuff can do to you, especially if you're around it all the time like I am. But we couldn't talk to each other anymore, and I felt certain somebody'd been coming to the house while I was gone. I could sense it, but I never said anything 'cause I couldn't be sure it wasn't just me. I came home one time and thought I could smell a cigar, and another time it smelled heavy and sweet, like somebody'd been smoking a pipe. I had this feeling, but what the hell does that mean? Carol went on like nothing had happened. She hummed over the sink while she did the dinner dishes, but I knew there were things she wasn't saying.

I beat her up pretty bad. I'm ashamed of that, but it's over. She called me Marion; she knew I hated that. It's what's on my birth certificate, but nobody calls me Marion. People call me Bobby. That's what it says on my business card: Bobby Huntoon, Charter Flights, Instruction, Agricultural Specialist. I'm what you'd call a crop duster. I never did fly in the service. You had to have been to college to fly in the military, but it was those World War II movies, and Korea, that first gave me the bug. I loved to watch the dogfights with Hellcats and those

27

gull-wing Corsairs. I don't think there was ever a prettier airplane, or ever will be.

I did a lot of different things after high school, motor tuneups, landscaping, farm work, but I never knew what I really wanted until seven years ago when I saw that Bearcat, the day before the first airshow at Brainard Municipal. I had this job laying sod around the new operations building, and late one afternoon when I went inside to get a drink of water, I heard Nolan Diggs on the unicom, talking with this pilot up at ten thousand feet. He was right overhead, he said, and coming down. "If it's clear," he said, "I'll make a run."

I didn't know what he was talking about, but I could tell Diggs knew. "Go to it," he said into the microphone. "No reported traffic. I'll keep a watch out."

Diggs ran the operation there and was airport manager for the city. Forty years ago he was a war hero and one hellacious pilot. He flew a Dauntless dive bomber at Midway and made a direct hit on a Japanese carrier. There's a picture of him in his leathers on the wall behind the desk. Leather helmet and all. I've met a lot of pilots all over the country who knew Diggs.

So after he cleared that pilot, he put down the mike, and we went outside. "You're gonna see something now, kid," he said. I couldn't see anything right then, but I was excited 'cause I could feel that Diggs was excited. He looked straight up in the sky and shielded his eyes from the sun. I looked up too, but all I could see were some high cumulus clouds and a few patches of blue. Then I heard a little burble of engine noise, and I spotted a tiny dark thing in one of those breaks in the clouds. "I know this guy," Diggs said. He didn't know me then.

I was just a kid laying sod for the city, but he wanted somebody to share this with. I looked up again and the spot was gone, and then a minute later Diggs pointed off to the east, just as I heard the engine again. The pilot was making big circles as he came down, and Diggs seemed to be chuckling inside himself. The airplane had disappeared again, and I was just about to go back to my sod truck when Diggs grabbed my shoulders and jerked me around. I heard that growl building up, and there it was, that Navy Bearcat with the stars and bars, diving straight down like something I'd seen in *Flying Leathernecks*. We heard the voice from the unicom speaker, talking calm like he was giving a bus tour. "Clear the decks, Diggs, I haven't lost it yet. Clean sweep, clean sweep," he said. How he could have talked like that with the G's he must've been pulling is something I still don't know for sure, but I could hear the scream of the wind off his wings like I'd heard just before an explosion when a fighter was going down in the movies, and I felt my legs start quivering.

"Hee, hee," Diggs laughed, like a little kid, and as that Bearcat hit the end of the runway, it pulled out about twenty feet off the deck and roared past us at over 400 miles an hour. "Jesus!" I thought about how it must've scared the shit out of the Japs on Iwo Jima to see something like that coming at them, 'cause it scared the shit out of me just watching. It was so much bigger and so much louder than I thought it would be in real life that I just started screaming for joy. The grass along the strip blew back like a hurricane hit it, and the Bearcat pulled up and did four snap-rolls, pop, pop, pop, pop, just like that and climbed out almost as straight up as he'd come down. I let out one big deep breath, and I looked at Diggs, and I knew right then that that's what I wanted to do more than anything in the world.

I met the pilot when he circled around and landed. He was an old Navy man like Diggs, and I didn't ask him, but I knew he must've flown at Midway too. He let me step up on the wing and take a look in the cockpit. It was a mystery to me, all those gauges and switches. "You want to fly her, boy?" Diggs laughed, and I just said, "Whew," or something like that, but I had my taste of it.

I started hanging around the airport all the time, doing anything I could that needed doing, and Diggs started giving me lessons. He told me I took to it natural, and when he had me home to dinner one night, I met his daughter, and it just all kind of fell into place.

I NEVER DID MEET CAROL'S MOTHER. The story was that Diggs had a big flight school down in southern Indiana, and that his wife took off with one of his instructors. I heard that from pilots I met around the country while I was flying charters. Carol told me her mother was dead. Carol was always her daddy's girl, and she laughed a lot there at first. She was a grown woman, but she'd never been anywhere or done anything. She'd sit on her Daddy's lap and call him Diggs. It was like he was afraid he might lose her too and wanted to hide her from the world. "Aw Diggy Poo," she'd say, and squeeze his face till he looked like a guppy. "You're awful sexy for a man your age," she'd say, "the best daddy there is in the world," stuff like that. I was kind of embarrassed to tell you the truth, but I laughed when she did it. And Diggs would smile, and you could see he loved it. I never imagined people carried on like that. I never knew families could be that way.

Diggs took me into the business with him, and when I got good enough, he started me in dusting crops. I got certified and took over the whole Ag end of the business, and a couple of years later, Carol and I got married. I'd had a few girls, but they were mostly just ones that whored around. I never really thought too much about it. It seemed like Carol came as part of the package. I was working with Diggs, and Carol fixed our supper every night. It was long hard days all spring and summer, but I loved it. I'd make a run, come back, tank up and go out again maybe fifteen or twenty times a day. I'd get so I could hardly stand up, and some of those chemicals smelled like pure rot. But it was like being in the movies half the time. I was spraying crops, but in my mind I was strafing Japs or the Cong. Sometimes I'd have to dive that Steerman under power lines to hit a field just right, or I'd bank up out of a blueberry marsh to cut the spray before I hit a lake or a cornfield. The DNR can get real nasty about that, and nobody appreciates a spray job they haven't contracted for.

Maybe if we'd had kids it would've been different. But Carol had one miscarriage and then she didn't want to try anymore. So she didn't have anything to do but wait around for me and watch TV. She was beautiful when I first met her, and she still could be when she'd get herself together, but that didn't happen very often. Maybe she just got bored, I don't know. It was like sleep got to be some kind of a disease for her. She started spending more and more time in bed. She'd sleep till noon and then lie there and watch soap operas, and most of the time she looked like the wrath of God when I'd come home for supper. Sometimes she wouldn't get up till three or four o'clock in the afternoon. I don't think she needed more sleep than anybody else. It was just that she couldn't stand very much time awake.

We had our own place, a farmhouse on the other side of the airport from where Diggs lived. He was sorry to see us move, and I wonder if maybe it wasn't a big mistake because that's when it started to go bad. Things got done around the house, things that had to be done, but just barely. And for a while there she wanted sex almost every night, but I didn't need that. She looked like a wreck, one of those whores I used to run around with. Maybe it was watching all those soap operas. She couldn't think of any other way to kill time till she could go back to sleep. Diggs was talking about retiring, and I had stuff to do nights, paper work, chemical mixes to figure out. It's not just fun and games. It's a business, and you got to be responsible for what you spray.

WHEN YOU LIVE ON THE EDGE, you're hot, and women are attracted to that. It's not like being a farmer or a salesman. When I go to a bar, I pick up on that right away. I don't fool around, not near as much as I could. Sometimes it's enough just knowing what's available. People know what I do. They can hear me over their fields all summer long. Sometimes I'm not more than five feet off the dirt when I'm laying down dimethoate or parathion, so close, one little unexpected downdraft would put you into the farm, screwed the pooch, as those test pilots say it.

I take risks all day. I'd come home and there'd be Carol, her face all puffy from sleep, her hair wild, looking like a witch. For a while there she stopped coming on to me, and she started to fix herself up again, doing her hair and wearing makeup, and that's when I started to wonder if she might not be seeing someone else. When I thought about it, I could feel it as sure as my pulse. She sure wasn't fixing herself up for me.

I started keeping an eye out. I'd make runs back over the house sometimes while I was giving a lesson or coming back to tank up for another spray run, a kind of aerial reconnaissance. I didn't come so close as to be conspicuous, and I don't know what might've gone on while I was away on a charter, but I thought about what I'd do when I found someone there. I figured I'd tank up with undiluted parathion and fly a pattern where I could just keep his car in sight, and when he came out of the house, buckling his belt, I'd dive out of the sun and give him a dose of cancer. I thought about stuff like that a lot, and maybe I got a little bit crazy.

I didn't tell Diggs about what I suspected, but we did talk about her sleeping all the time, and he didn't know what to make of it any more than I did. She didn't have training for any kind of job, and she wouldn't have gone out to look for one anyway. I got on her about that the night she called me Marion. God how I hate that name. I hated my mother for coming up with it. She never got married, and when she found out she was pregnant, she wanted me to be a girl. She used to tell people that, "I wanted a girl, but I got this." I remember at least once her whacking me on the ear when she said it. She was talking to some whore in the supermarket, and when she said "this," she slapped me, hard, like it was my fault. "Marion." I can still hear her voice when she said it, sharp and ugly, the way someone might say "asshole." I think she gave me that name to get even, and when she died of pneumonia the year before I met Diggs, I didn't cry one tear.

I think maybe I was hearing my mother that night when I pounded on Carol. She started coming on to me, the first time in months, and it was pitiful. I was tired, and I'd been having a little bit to drink. She was going on in a whiny voice about how I never paid her any attention anymore, and I said, "Maybe it's because you don't pay yourself any attention anymore. What are you? You lay around like a turd all day. You're about as sexy as dirty laundry." I came down pretty hard. And then she said maybe I just wasn't a man anymore. "I think that's just an excuse is what I think," she said. "You wouldn't be nobody if it wasn't for my dad, and you're just afraid to admit it. Marion's the right name for you," she said, "'cause that's about how much good you are as a man." She started laughing like it was the funniest thing in the world, and that's when I cut her off. I hit her right in the mouth, and I hit her one more time as she was going down. She fell on her hands and knees like she was looking for something on the floor, and she started bleeding all over the linoleum. I could hear the blood dripping like water from a pan, and for a minute I felt good about it. She didn't cry or anything. She just watched the blood pooling up on the floor, and then she looked up at me with no expression at all, like I might've been the soft-water man, who walked in on her while she was scrubbing the kitchen floor.

I stood there and watched her for maybe half a minute. And

then I said to myself, Bobby Huntoon, who are you? That woman on the floor was like someone I'd never seen. I got a wet towel, and I cleaned her up and got her in the car. We didn't say anything all the way over to Diggs' house.

"I brought your daughter back home," I said when he came to the door, and he took her in just like that. He put his arms around her. He said, "Thank you." And then he said good night, and he closed the door. I stood there on his porch for a little while and watched my breath steam out in the chilly summer night. I thought of the first night I came there, and I felt like something was over. Then I stepped down off the porch, and I walked back to my car. I had to be at the airport at first light the next morning. I had four hundred acres of celery to spray before the ground started to warm and the breeze came up.

A DAPPER

LITTLE MAN

A dapper little man. That's how she described him. She didn't say what he was wearing, but I can guess. He wouldn't have spats, no, not today, but probably those two-tone wingtip shoes, brown and white, that amount to the same thing, and one of those pinched-up little hats with a too-narrow brim, the kind with a tiny red feather in the side. She said he was so nice she wanted to invite him in for a drink. But I'm getting ahead of myself here.

The truth is Sunny's kind of gone downhill since the divorce. She just seemed to get rough around the edges, her clothes a little sloppy, her hair a little frizzy, like she didn't use a mirror anymore. And that surprises me too. You'd think it might work the other way. I know it would with me. She let the house go too, all kind of lifeless and messy. But she could see that all around her, and she just wasn't raised that way. So that's when she hired Mrs. Wabeke to come in and clean twice a week. She could afford it. She got a good settlement off Harold, and he could afford it. His picture would be in the paper every year for selling over a million dollars of insurance. Still, I've never understood why she married him. She had too much spirit for an insurance man. We were in 4-H together.

Well, it happened while Sunny was out. She works part-time at the Co-op, doing the books for the end of the month. Sunny had a lot of parties after Harold left, you know, intimate little gatherings. And Mrs. Wabeke was there cleaning up, just Mrs. Wabeke and Sunny's three cats, Muffin, Skipper, and Squirt. Mrs. Wabeke likes cats. I know she does. And she watches soap operas while she cleans. I've been there. Sunny was helping me with my income tax. She's good at that. And Mrs. Wabeke was vacuuming the living room carpet, and over it all we could hear "The Edge of Night," clear out in the kitchen. Anyway, this afternoon I was talking about, Mrs. Wabeke was there alone, and she picked up Muffin, or Squirt maybe. No, it was Muffin. I know because Muffin's the one with the little white mustache-like mark around her mouth that makes her look like Hitler. Probably just stroking her while "General Hospital" came to a good part, and Muffin bit her. She would do that. She had a mind of her own. She could be real loving, but when she'd had enough, she'd had enough. She just bit and scrammed.

Mrs. Wabeke was real surprised, but she didn't think much of it till she got home and saw how her hand had begun to swell and get red around the bite marks, little red lines shooting up toward her wrist and across her knuckles. That's when she got concerned and called Sunny. Could the cat have rabies or what? You don't fool around with stuff like that. Last year, right here in our town, a woman walked into her nursery and found a bat biting her baby. She had the presence of mind to catch the bat—I don't know how she did though—and kept it for the Health Department up in White Cloud. Imagine finding a bat

37

on your baby. Well, the Health Department found out the bat was okay, and then so was the baby. But if she hadn't checked it out, she'd have never known, and if the baby'd died of rabies, she'd have felt terrible.

So Sunny called the Health Department, and they told her that all they'd need was the cat's head to check it out for rabies. That was a laugh. Sunny almost cracked up. I was there when she called. "Well, the cat just happens to be alive," she told them, "and I don't think she'd much appreciate your checking out her head without taking the rest of her along too." It was funny to be there and see the look on her face. She winked at me when she said it, and I'll bet the Health Department guy was a little set back. Sunny can be a card. "Well, quarantine the cat," the Health Department guy told her, and they'd be by to pick it up in three days. That's when they'd be able to tell about the rabies. At least that's what Sunny told me they said.

Well, we were having coffee, and how do you quarantine a cat? we wondered. Then right away we saw the Big Wheel box on the counter. Sunny and I had just come back from the store. That was it. She put the cat in the Big Wheel box and covered it with her Ouija board. It was a big heavy wooden board, the same one she'd predicted I'd marry Gerald Sykes on, but it never happened. Gerald went to Colorado, some real estate deal out there. I wonder if I ever will get married or, after all I've seen Sunny put up with, if I ever want to, really. I'd like a man once in a while, but I don't think they're any fun to live with. Gerald could sure make me happy though, when he wanted to. He could say just the right things, and there were times in bed when I couldn't think of anything else or why anybody'd ever want to think of anything else. And for a while there I thought the Ouija board was going to make it happen for me and Gerald, but later Sunny figured out how she'd done something wrong with the planchette, held it wrong, or—I don't know how those things work. It wasn't the board's fault, she said, but Gerald left town the morning of the night the tornado tore through the south side and made confetti of the trailer where we had slept the very night before. When it was all over, I don't know if I was more shook up about Gerald's leaving or wondering what if that twister'd hit one night sooner, because it killed Mrs. Jennings in the trailer right next door, pitched her into the water-treatment plant where they didn't find her till two days later 'cause it didn't occur to them to look for her there. And a lot of people didn't drink the water for the next few days. I never heard from Gerald either, except one little postcard where he said, "Oh my darling I'm so glad you're safe." That was all, after a year fooling around together, and on a postcard too. I've never wanted to mess with Ouija boards again either. That twister was a terrible thing, you can't imagine. And we'd never had one in the county before, that I ever heard of.

So I felt a little funny when she covered that box with the Ouija board, but then we were talking about what a shock it was that Garret Scotiers, president of the Brainard State Bank, had been caught embezzling the trust fund for the Methodist Church because he had a mistress in Grand Rapids. We knew he did, but to have it all come out like that. That's what was on our minds.

Well, there it was, the cat in the box under the Ouija board, and one thing led to another. And it was three days later when Sunny and I were at Shop 'n' Save that it hit her. "Oh my God," she said. We were in the delicatessen section, trying to figure out if the cheeses they had there were really any different from those they had in the dairy case or just repackaged and marked up. These merchants take us for fools sometimes. And "Oh my God," she says, "Muffin." She dropped the cheese, and we left the half-full cart right there in the aisle and ran for the parking lot.

Muffin was dead when we got there, and of course Sunny felt terrible about it but then figured maybe it'd been the rabies, and that's how we'd find out. She called the Health Department right away, and they said they'd be over that afternoon. But it wasn't a half an hour later, Sunny told me—I'd left right after that—that the doorbell rang, and there was that dapper little man. "Good morning, Madam. I've come for the cat," he said, and tipped his hat. I don't know what else he said, but Sunny said he was so charming she almost didn't want to let him get away. She offered him some coffee, and he said that was very kind but that he had a schedule to keep and was running a bit behind. They must've said some personal things, Sunny didn't say, but she just couldn't stop talking about how nice he was. He said all he'd need was the cat's head, but she said how she'd prefer that he take the whole cat. She showed him where Muffin was under the Ouija board, and before she could even open her mouth, she said, he whipped out a knife, lopped off Muffin's head and dropped it in a black bag he pulled out of his pocket. "Thank you kindly, Madam," he said and tipped his hat again and was gone before Sunny could say jackshit. Excuse me, but that's how it was. She thought he was charming, she said, but can you imagine that headless cat there in her kitchen? She said she just sat down and poured herself a drink of Southern Comfort, and about the time she'd got the second one down, there was the doorbell again. She straightened herself up, and I know Sunny, she doesn't make a habit of drinking midday. She went to the door, and there were these two big men in white coats. They looked kind of young, she said, but they said to her, "We're here for the cat."

Well, Sunny just started laughing. "You're kidding," she said. "You were just here not half an hour ago."

"No ma'am," the bigger one said. "You must be mistaken. We got the call on the CB just before lunch."

"Ha," was all that Sunny said, "you're the ones that's mistaken." She said she just took the big one by the sleeve of his white coat and led him right to the kitchen. "There's the cat," she said. You can just picture her standing there, a little bit tipsy, with the Ouija board in her hand and those two big hunks from the Health Department. "There's the cat, or what's left of it, and you people came and took off her head."

Well, those guys couldn't figure it out. And then she said the big one looked at her real funny, like he'd smelled something bad, and by then I'm sure the cat was getting pretty ripe. So he looked at her and said, "Who came? What did he look like?"

"Ha," Sunny laughed again, and she told them about the dapper little man with the knife and the black bag in his pocket. And that's when it hit 'em, she said. The big one looked at the not-so-big one and said, "Not again!" and they looked like this was some kind of nightmare they were having. "This has happened before," they told her. Every time there was a cat involved, the same little man with the same knife and black bag. They left shaking their heads, she said, and they didn't even think to take what was left of the cat.

Well, Mrs. Wabeke was all right, so I guess it wasn't rabies. Sunny was relieved about that. And she still talks about the dapper little man and how charming he was. She talks about that more than what happened, really. Little men especially can be that way sometimes. Gerald wasn't very big himself. I heard through his Aunt Reya he'd moved on to New Mexico. I still think about him sometimes. We had a tornado watch last week. The sky turned all green and yellow, but finally it just rained. Sunny and I still wonder about that little man. You'd think I'd have met him if he lived around here. I look around when I'm in town. I know I'll see him one of these days.

ONE MORNING
IN MAY

"I don't know, Tom," he said. "I just don't know." He'd called to tell me that Denise had left him. Oh Christ, I thought. Why me? I'd promised to take Chris and Troy fishing, and that was the first thing I thought of as I was waking up. I watched the sky while Larry talked. It looked sunny one minute and cloudy the next, but the wind was out of the west, and that was a good sign.

We used to have a martin house on a pole in the yard, but every spring it got taken over by grackles and our patio served as a convenient target for them, to the point that we considered just painting the bricks white. So this spring I took the martin house down. Carolyn bought a blue and green nylon banner at a kite store, and I hung it on the pole. It looks a little quiche, I think, a little yuppy, like golfers with green pants, but it tells me which way the wind's blowing. If it's coming out of the east, you can forget fishing. I don't know why that is, but it's true.

So here we go again, I thought, the Larry and Denise Show. She hadn't actually left him, he explained. She'd kicked him out of the house. He'd come home late and found a suitcase full of clothes on the front porch. And a note taped to it saying, "Have a nice life."

"That's it?" I asked.

"That's it."

I'd often wondered if he and Denise didn't just go at it as a form of amusement. But this time his voice cracked as he told me about it.

"There was an old box of letters there too," he added.

"What kind of letters?" I'd been working hard all week up on the ladder, and it'd been hot. I didn't need this kind of crap on a Saturday.

"Old letters. From Lynn Smith."

"How old?"

"Years old. Ancient history."

Lynn was a woman Larry had a thing with a few years ago. He met her in a night class when he was building up credits for his masters. He had a drink with her one night after class, and they started going over to her apartment. Since we were kids, I've always admired the decisiveness with which Larry moves, a boldness that half-frightened me to imagine in my own life, but which I also envied. He told me Lynn was easily the most enthusiastic lay he'd ever had, and that for a while he thought he was in love with her. But it was probably just because she was good for his ego. Larry had been playing Mr. Chips. He would volunteer for just about anything, junior class sponsor, Homecoming, yearbook, direct the school play. He'd gotten some idea about being "good," as if he were trying for the Most Beloved Teacher award. He'd been carrying that virtuous, long-suffering look around on his face. Not the Larry I knew and envied.

So when he started this thing with Lynn Smith, it was like

44

having the real Larry back again. He told me how they would laugh out loud while they were fucking for the sheer joy of it. "We just dropped all pretenses and went at it," he told me. "It's so honest. She wants me and I want her. We just explode together."

He said it was like candy, and he couldn't get enough. They talked on the phone during the week between classes, and they wrote to each other. "We could say things in letters we couldn't say over the phone. I gave myself up completely," he said. "I felt like a poet." He had her write him at the high school so Denise wouldn't see the strange envelopes. But eventually she found out. Larry couldn't contain himself. He was getting so much joy out of it, he told me, that he just had to share it with Denise. "I just knew anything that felt that right couldn't be wrong," he told me.

I think maybe it was the guilt that got to him. He said he wanted to live existentially toward everyone, whatever that means. He told Denise it had nothing to do with her. He told her his seeing Lynn made him love her even more and that he knew she'd really like Lynn if she just got to know her.

But Denise didn't want to get to know Lynn, and Larry was crushed. He thought they could all three love each other equally. That was back during Quaaludes, and before AIDS, when love came pretty easy. Of course he was crazy, but I figured anyone could get crazy once in their life. He got the ultimatum, and he caved in. He said he came to realize that what he had with Denise had stood the test of time and that he could probably never really trust Lynn Smith anyway. If she fell for him so easily, he reasoned, she might get it on with anyone. I also think at that point it occurred to him that Denise's money from her father made the payments on their house and on his Pontiac Grand-Am.

Anyway, that all ended five or six years ago, and they seemed like they had started all over again. For a year or so after Larry broke it off with Lynn, he and Denise didn't even fight, at least not in public. But eventually they got back to normal. Carolyn and I were with them last weekend at the Hoppers' anniversary party, and they were in rare form. It was all about whether or not Larry took his share of responsibility for their daughters, Melissa and Mindy. Christ, I'll never understand why anyone would name a kid Mindy. I mean, someday she'll be sixty years old, and she'll still be called Mindy.

So there was this box of letters on the porch with his suitcase and the note from Denise.

"You mean you kept them all this time?"

"They're part of my life, Tom," he pleaded. "I couldn't just pretend it never happened."

"Have you got rocks for brains?" I asked him. It was Saturday morning. I just wanted to go fishing and forget about painting houses. I was also going to be fulfilling my parental responsibility, so it just wasn't that I didn't want to get involved. But I had to say something.

"Where will you go?" I asked. It seemed the most logical question.

"Home, I guess. Over to my mother's house. I'm all alone now."

Oh give me a break, I thought. "Look, I promised Chris and Troy I'd take them fishing today." I was glad I had that to fall back on, though when I made the promise last Wednesday, I'd thought of it as a kind of an imposition on my weekend. I mean I wanted to go fishing, but I wanted some time alone, too. I'd rather just take a couple of six-packs out on the lake and drown a few worms. But with the kids along, that was out. They go fishing to catch fish. I can't get real stupid on beer and do that. And Carolyn would really get pissed if I drank more than one or two beers in front of the boys. So now I could be a good father and not willfully shirk my responsibility as a friend.

"Your mother's?" I said. "That sounds like a good idea." I couldn't think of anything else to say that wouldn't get me involved. Larry's mother died of cancer last February. I helped Larry move her furniture out of her house a week after the funeral, before he put it on the market, and it had stood empty all spring.

"I guess I've got a lot to think about," Larry moaned. "So much has happened. I just wonder if it matters."

"If what matters?" Oh Christ, I thought.

"Anything. Life. I don't know. It just seems like some kind of cosmic joke. We deal with all this shit, and then we die."

"That's what we do, all right. Of course we could just die," I said, and then wished I hadn't.

"Look, Tom, I'm sorry to unload all this on you. I guess I'm being kind of a jerk about it." His voice was wistful and a little hoarse.

"No, you're not being a jerk," I lied. "It's just that things look bleak right now. They'll change." I waited for some response, but he didn't say anything. "Look, I'll call you at your mother's house tonight, when I get back from fishing."

47

"I don't have a phone."

"Well, I'll come by then, and we'll talk about it."

"Okay, Tom." His voice had that plummy, overly sincere quality it takes on sometimes. "You're a true friend. And thanks. It means a lot."

Oh, don't say that, I thought. Christ, a true friend. I'm not going to let this ruin my day, I told myself. It's probably just teaching that's got him down. I taught for seven years. I had to quit to keep from going batshit. It can take over your soul, casting hard-earned wisdom on a sea of acned indifference, getting all wrapped up in the traumas of adolescence and putting up with all the crap from parents and the administration. It's not really living like an adult. He'd feel a lot better in a few weeks when school's out, I thought. Painting houses can be a bitch too, especially when it's hot like it was this past week, but at least I stay sane. Sometimes it's pretty nice. I tune in the classical music station on the FM, and I can think my own thoughts. I don't make as much as Carolyn does running the day care center at the hospital, but I don't have any hang-ups about it.

I STARTED THINKING ABOUT LARRY again while I was out on the lake with the boys. We had a pretty good run of luck early on. They each caught a half-dozen bluegills and a couple of small perch. Then we got into a lull toward noon. We ran out of bites, and the boys ran out of questions. I thought about how Larry had really seemed to pull himself together over the winter, dealing with his mother's dying. It was a pretty rough scene. Bone cancer. They had her in the hospital, but there wasn't anything they could do, just feed her morphine through an I.V. and look after her bedsores. She wanted to come home, so Larry got her a nurse. I think Denise paid for it. She liked Larry's mother. Vera was a remarkable woman, especially near the end. For all her suffering, she made you think the worst life had to offer wasn't so bad. I went to see her almost every week. She could nearly make you believe dying was easy. It was kind of inspiring. But I could see through it. She couldn't hide the pain. Her skin looked like tissue paper, and all her tendons stood out, like in those photos of Dachau. But there was a light in her eyes, like there was something we couldn't see. She even made Larry forget himself for a while. She could barely move her head or her hands, and couldn't move her legs at all, and Larry just couldn't do enough for her. I thought it had brought about a real change in him, that he couldn't be so self-indulgent anymore. I don't really believe in that sort of thing, but it seemed like he was having some kind of religious experience.

I remember him holding her hand as she lay in that big bed, so shriveled up she seemed lost in it. Can you find the woman in this picture? And he sang to her, songs she must have sung when he was a child. His voice wasn't much more than a kind of mumbling, but it was a pretty touching thing to see, and it seemed to ease her pain. I remember him sitting there, still croaking those songs for maybe an hour or more after she was gone.

And then I thought about how his voice had sounded on the telephone that morning when he told me he was going home. And I thought, what's home? Where do you go finally? I mean *finally*. I was sure there was more to it than he let on. Denise might've found those letters from Lynn, but that was probably just the icing on the cake. I can't make excuses about Larry. He can be a real jerk-off. But I thought about him sitting alone in that room where his mother died. You can't really make assumptions about people. I couldn't honestly say that Larry wasn't the kind of person who might do anything. I got to thinking that he must've felt as if the earth had been pulled out from under him.

THE FISHING PICKED UP again later on, and the boys were happy. Chris had been irritated with Troy's ineptitude at getting the fish off his hook and his squeamishness about putting a new worm on. But as the afternoon wore on, he grew more patient and showed Troy how to take a hold of the fish without getting stabbed by its dorsal fin and how to work the stringer through its gills. Troy felt better about himself, handling his own fish, and Chris was proud about having been able to teach him. I stayed out of it as much as I could because I thought it would be good to let them work it out together, and because I'd had a few more beers, and I was feeling a little dreamy.

There was a breeze over the water, and the points of sunlight flashing off the ripples had sort of hypnotized me. I drowsed into a kind of half-sleep where I didn't really care about fishing, and after a while I stopped even baiting my hook. I just sat there happily watching the boys watching their bobbers. I watched other boats on other parts of the lake. Occasionally a kingfisher or a gull would glide over the water, and I saw a great blue heron lumber over the distant shore like a transport plane coming in for a landing. I don't know if it was that vision of the heron or if it might've been the dragonflies, which appeared like tiny helicopters, in tandem just above the water, that made me think of Viet Nam and how often, over there, I thought of being home on the lake, spending an afternoon just like this one.

I'd had a lot of time in Nam with nothing to do but to think about what the guys I knew back home might be doing. I don't think I was really alive while I was there. I was in a kind of a holding pattern, just counting the days and minutes till my time would be up. I don't mean I don't have any memories from that time. It's just that they're mostly things I put together after I got back home, things that might be true. But that doesn't matter.

I spent four months at a supply depot near Cu Chi, doing nothing. I was in charge of keeping an inventory of everything that came in by C-130 and records and requisitions of what went out by chopper or of what just got carried away. This was in '69 when we were trying to get the Vietnamese to take over more of the war so that eventually we could go home. That was the idea anyway. So this depot was under joint command: me, a lieutenant, and an A.R.V.N. captain. But those A.R.V.N. guys didn't care any more about history than we did. I don't know what they cared about. Being back home was a different thing for them than it was for us. They must've had wives and girl-friends they thought about. But they didn't think about win-ning the war. These guys were like watchdogs in a butcher shop. The captain would present me with requisitions for ciga-rettes and beer, all scratched out on the proper forms, in Viet-namese so I couldn't read them. But he'd explain it to me.

"Okay, Lutenut, this mean 200 box cigarettes, 50 box beer for Bin Lau."

Cooperate with the South Vietnamese. Encourage their taking the initiative. That was the word that came down to us, but that A.R.V.N. captain didn't need any encouragement. And he had rank on me. He'd bring a platoon of his men over to my warehouse and they'd carry off supplies like army ants. You'd think there was a big offensive being fought with soap and beer. Those C-130s would bring it in, and the A.R.V.N. choppers would haul it out, right back to Saigon where our guys could buy it back with greenbacks.

And we were friends at the time. I remember sitting around a campfire getting high with the captain and some of his men. Except for the captain, they didn't have any English, and I didn't have any Vietnamese, so I don't remember what we talked about. We couldn't have talked about anything, but we laughed a lot. It was the only response that made any sense, and the pot we had there was much stronger than any I've had since. The captain generously shared some of the beer he'd requisitioned from me, and we were as happy as pigs in shit, which is about as apt a metaphor as I can think of.

I remember that one night there was this rat that joined our group around the fire. He came into the circle just like another grunt and sat there staring at the fire. He had as much to say as any of us did. I can't remember him laughing out loud, but I can't remember that he didn't, either. He just sat there like one of the boys until the captain burned him on the ass with a cigarette. He bent over the rat and talked to it as if it were a child, as if he were saying, "Oh little rat, do you want to be a soldier, too? We have plenty of beer here to share with you. The Americans are very generous. We'll make you a general." Then he saluted it, and then he jabbed it in the ass. The rat made a quick jump in the air and scurried back into the darkness. We all laughed about that, but I remember now that I thought it was a mean thing to do, even to a rat.

I DON'T KNOW WHY that still mattered to me, or why I would get pissed off thinking about that embezzled beer there on the lake where everything was just the way I wanted it to be. Because it hadn't bothered me at the time. I just saluted and said, "Take it away." Those were my orders. Maybe it was because I didn't want to think about Larry, but I couldn't get that keening edge in his voice out of my head. I knew better than to take Larry seriously, but I thought about how things can build up, a death in the family, a rejection by someone you love. Those are heavy things. And I thought about suicides, how they were often the last people their friends suspected. I thought about it that night while we were cleaning the fish, while I was cutting off their heads, watching their eyes bulge under the pressure of the knife, and pulling their guts out after I'd slit them up the middle from vent to gills. Pretty physical stuff. And I wasn't feeling red hot. All that beer out in the hot sun, and I was ready for bed before it even got dark.

It had been a good day. Carolyn was happy because the boys were happy. They were getting along better than they normally did. Carolyn said she was proud of me and thanked me for showing the boys a good time. And she came to bed in her black lace teddy, a definite signal. I hope it wasn't just gratitude.

Sunday morning I felt fine. No hangover. I didn't even think about Larry until after we'd had our celebratory breakfast of fried bluegills and popovers. Carolyn mentioned that a pair of Larry's shorts had turned up in our laundry, and I remembered that I'd borrowed a pair from him when we'd decided to wash our cars over at his house the previous weekend. And then I remembered that I'd promised to come by and see him when I got home from fishing, and I'd forgotten all about it. Death, rejection, abandonment by your friends. I heard the strained quality of his voice again, and I thought of him alone in that house where he'd been through the long winter of his mother's dying.

"Times like this, you get to know who your friends are," I could hear him saying.

I got stopped on my way over to his house. Forty in a twenty-five zone, two points on my license and a thirty-dollar fine. I thought about trying to explain to the cop, but I wouldn't have known where to begin. In an odd way I was glad about the ticket. It would be something I could complain about if Larry started his poor waif routine.

I parked across the street and looked over at the house. It had a gaunt, spooky look to it, the tall, curtained windows of the second story, the deserted porch, the uncut grass, a house where horrible things might've happened, or might happen still. The kind of house that invited kids to throw stones at it. It needs paint, I thought, and I caught myself beginning to figure an estimate. Larry's Grand-Am was at the curb in front, and it was covered with shed blossoms from the flowering crabs. Obviously it hadn't been moved for some time.

I felt a chill as I walked up onto the porch. It was dead quiet, and the paint on the floorboards was flaking. I almost didn't want to breathe. The dark stained wood on that bright May morning made the front door seem foreboding, as if I might step through it into my worst nightmares.

"Bullshit," I said to myself. "This is Larry Rafferty we're talking about." But I began to feel queasy again when, after five series of knocks on the door, there was no response. He had to be there. He wouldn't have gone back home and left his car.

The doorknob felt cold in my hand, and the door opened silently. It was too quiet and too dark in the front hall. Maybe it was this house that had made Larry so morose, I thought, the walls, all dark paneling, the bookshelves empty. The sunlight through the drawn blinds cast a yellow pall in the empty rooms. It was hard to imagine, in the surrounding neighborhood, chiropractors in bathrobes drinking coffee over the Sunday comics, covering "The Flintstones" and "Doonesbury" with thumbprints of butter and jam, haberdashers and their wives singing "Onward Christian Soldiers," high school seniors addressing graduation announcements. Nothing of that world in here.

The oak stair treads didn't even creak under my feet. I climbed up through the near darkness and turned at the landing. I was imagining what I might find at the top of the stairs and paused on the landing to catch my breath. I hadn't climbed more than a dozen steps, but I could feel my temples pulsing. You son of a bitch, I thought. I don't need this.

And then I heard something that wasn't me. I heard a board creak from the upstairs hallway, and then I heard it again. I took a deep breath, all the way down to my navel, and thought how my imagination might kill me someday. "Larry?" I called out. "Larry?"

"Who is it? Who's there?" The voice came down to me out of the darkness. It was a hoarse whisper, like orange juice full of pulp, and I realized it wasn't Larry's voice.

"Tom," I said softly.

"Oh, Tom," the voice said, as if it knew me as an old friend. "Larry's sleeping, but come on up."

It was a girl, or woman, wherever you draw the line. She was about chin high on me, and she smelled of sleep. A light from a window I couldn't see made a frizzy halo around her wild hair. "What time is it, anyway?" she asked.

"About eleven o'clock." I wanted to ask who she was, but it seemed presumptuous.

"This way," she said. "Can you see?"

I was going to tell her that I knew the house, but she had already taken my hand and was leading me toward the light of the doorway of what had been Larry's mother's room.

"There's no electricity," she said. "We just about broke our goddamned necks on the stairs last night."

Her hand was awfully small. A child's hand, I thought. In the bedroom, I could see that she was wearing a man's shirt and apparently nothing else. She let go of my hand and went over to the bed where she knelt on the sheet and shook the body I assumed was Larry's.

"Yeh, yeh," he said, startled, and then, "Ooh," as his arms reached up for her.

"Somebody's here," she said. I could see her holding him away as he tried to pull her down to the mattress.

56

"Huh?" He rose up on his elbows. "Tom? Oh, Tom! Hey Tom, how're you doing?"

"Fine," I said. I was doing fine. I was relieved, I guess.

"Oh," Larry said again. "What time is it?"

"Eleven," I said again, feeling at least useful.

The woman got off the bed and bent to pull the cord of the blind at the window. She jerked it a couple of times and let it roll about halfway up, and I had a chance to confirm that the shirt was all she was wearing before the spring sunlight came flooding in to temporarily blind me.

Larry had pulled himself up and propped a pillow against the brass headboard of the bed in which his dying mother had lain as he croaked those lullabies.

"Isn't it a neat bed?" the girl-woman said, as if she were reading my mind.

"Yes," I nodded.

"I've seen beds like it in movies," she said. "I just couldn't believe it when I saw it right here."

"It's a nice bed, all right."

Larry was sitting there with a smile on his face, the same smile, it occurred to me, he had worn when he first showed me his new Grand-Am.

"Oh Tom," he said as an afterthought, "have you met Darlene?"

"We met in the hall," I said. "Nice to meet you, Darlene." There wasn't much to say after that. Darlene was stepping into a pair of cream-colored panties.

"Have you known Larry long?" I asked.

"Well, it seems like I have." She smiled and looked over at

Larry, who sat looking angelic and contented against the pillows of the bed. "It seems like we've known each other always," she said, "but we really only met last Wednesday at Sears."

"At Sears?"

"I work at Sears. Larry came in to buy a new chamois. We started feeling various chamois and talking about how soft they were. Did you ever experience a chamois, I mean *really* experience a chamois?" She laughed. "Larry and I found out just how soft a chamois can be." She looked at Larry rather than at me while she spoke, and he was looking at her. "And I think he's one happy customer."

"I'll bet he is," I said. I felt like a room service waiter, but I didn't have anything to do with my hands. Darlene was pretty, I decided.

"Well I said I'd stop by. Since you didn't have a phone," I explained.

"Hey, I'm glad you did," Larry said. He was the soul of self-satisfaction. "I'm glad you got to meet Darlene."

"So am I," I said.

"Why don't you call me later," Larry said. "Maybe we can shoot some hoops."

"You don't have a phone," I reminded him.

"That's right," he said, with a big grin on his face. "I'll call you, then." He was rubbing Darlene's neck as he spoke, the way you might absent-mindedly stroke the fur of a cat.

"Okay," I said. "I'll wait to hear from you."

THE STAIRS WERE ESPECIALLY DARK after the brightness of the bedroom. I groped my way down, feeling along the walls, remembering how I'd helped Larry move his mother's furniture down those stairs and wondering why it was we had left her bed. In the darkness there, nothing seemed quite what it was. I saw Carolyn and the boys, disembodied faces floating down before me, Denise and the suitcase, the grinning face of the A.R.V.N. captain at Cu Chi and those indifferent requisitions, scribbled in a language I couldn't read.

LORRAINE

Dewey makes his move, and I slip my piece over so that if he is paying attention he can jump me twice and be kinged. But he doesn't see it, and I pick up his checker and set it by the board, and I sigh.

There's a lot of sadness here. Almost every day we lose someone. Each morning at breakfast you look around to see who isn't there. They die or the light just goes out, and they drool off into oblivion. The nurses wheel them up to the TV room, but they don't talk anymore. Sometimes they are just left in the corridors with a bib around their necks.

One lady down the hall hollers, "Why, why, why," every afternoon, on and on like some tropical bird. It's sad. But there's some fun, and there are memories. Dewey lives across the hall with Mr. Brailis. Dewey and I were married for sixteen years. Then for forty-some years we hardly spoke. Now we play checkers almost every afternoon, and we talk. Funny how that's worked out. We've got no axes to grind anymore. We're both going to die, so why not be friends?

I'm an American now. That's how I think of myself. I have just a little accent left, and if someone asks, I say, U.S.A. But when I met Dewey I was French, though I thought of myself as Alsatian. We'd been German and French from week to week so many times, I didn't care. But when the Americans came we were French. They used our village for their headquarters, and the soldiers moved in with the families of the town. Some slept in barns, and some moved right into the houses. They were boys then, so innocent. We thought they were funny, shipped up on trains like they were going to camp, singing their songs, like cherubs. We'd had four years of it. We were like a soldiers' hotel, French and German. They'd come in and fall back, and whichever army was not our guest at the time would shell us, not heavy like in the trenches, but enough to keep us awake at night. And then the Americans came, like boy scouts, like this was a great adventure. But it didn't last long.

Dewey stayed with us when his company was relieved from the trenches. The sector was a quiet one, a *bel secteur*, the first weeks he was there, before the offensive began. He slept in the barn the first few times, and my father grew to like him. I was the only one in my family who spoke English, the little I had learned in school, but Dewey helped my father in the time he had free, and they had the language of work. Dewey was a sergeant then, and his captain was the first man in his regiment to be killed by the Germans. Dewey had been with him when they went to that forward observation post early in the morning. I learned all these terms from the soldiers, in three languages. The Americans talked the most because it was new to them. It was like they were telling you things they'd learned in school. Beautiful children. That's how I thought about Dewey, a beautiful child, so thin, so eager to defeat the *Boche* and save the world.

And he's a child now, so gentle with age. Men have a strange kind of courage, at least men like Dewey. They can throw themselves into danger, just turn off their minds and charge into battle, but the hardness of life is something else. Dewey won his medal, his Croix de Guerre, in a raid with the French on a town called Ammertzwiller, just about five miles from Soppe-le-Bas. I used to think in kilometers as a girl. Now that I have learned to think in miles, America is trying to teach everyone about kilometers. Last year I read in the paper where they put up a sign just south of Brainard with the distance to Grand Rapids in both kilometers and miles. Too bad I won't be around.

But Dewey was brave. He didn't know any better. The Americans were like that. They hadn't been pounded those terrible four years. The French soldiers, the *Pouli* or "Little Hairy Ones," had been numb since the fall of Verdun. We called the Americans *les terribles*, the terrible ones. Dewey charged in under a barrage of cannons and took German prisoners. He was probably still thinking about his captain, thinking of the *Boche* as evil beasts.

The Germans had been waiting for them in the trenches the morning his captain was killed. Dewey was right behind him when his captain was shot in the stomach. There were many German soldiers on both sides of the trench, and Dewey and the other sergeants fought their way back to their own lines. It was a miracle that they made it, Dewey told me. I was in love

with him, but not because of his bravery. It was his innocence
I loved. A child from a magic land, that's how I thought of him,
and I taught him about women one night in the loft of my
father's barn. He was so grateful, like I had given him a great
gift, and right away he wanted to marry me. I had never even
thought of that. He had a girl in Brainard, but I think they had
only kissed. I had been with French soldiers and German soldiers too. I was only nineteen, and any night a shell might blow
up our house, so what was the difference? There was no enemy
as far as we were concerned. I didn't tell Dewey about the others, and I think he would have not wanted to know. Some of
the men I was with may have killed each other. I used to wonder
about that.

I told Dewey that he was too young, that he didn't know me,
but he insisted he loved me, and when his regiment went back
to the Marne, he promised he would return for me. I think all
soldiers want some idea to hold on to. They marched out, and
I thought of him as another soldier who had come and gone.
And I think he was not so brave after that. I heard from his
comrades. He was still a good soldier at Château-Thierry and
Soissons, but he thought more about staying alive.

After the Armistice he came back to Belfort. I went there to
meet him, and we were married, just before he was shipped
back to America in December. Six months later he sent me
money to come join him, and he met my boat in New York. I
still couldn't quite believe it. He'd just gotten out of the army.
He had been in Waco, Texas, and we came back to Brainard
together. His family was so happy to have him home, they

didn't pay much attention to me at first. But I was quite a pretty girl then, and Mr. Brande, Dewey's father, liked me right away. I think I reminded him of Dewey's grandmother who had come from the Netherlands.

WE LIVED WITH HIS FAMILY that first year, but his mother was very cold to me. She had wanted Dewey to marry Clara Beckwith. She had planned for that since Dewey and Clara were children. Clara was the perfect girl for Dewey. And I think his mother was jealous of me because Mr. Brande loved me so. She tried to ignore me. She would make plans for Dewey and try to keep me out of them, like I was the immigrant girl brought in to clean toilets and wash windows. I didn't shed one tear when she died. I don't think Dewey could understand. He was blind to so much. Anything that didn't please him, he just didn't see. For a while I wondered if all Americans were that way, or was it just the men?

But Dewey's father faced life, and he treated me like a lady. I would have gone over to him after Dewey's mother died, if only he had asked. But that would have been unthinkable. He was in love with me, but he was a gentleman, always, though he kissed me once, or should I say I kissed him. This was ten years after I'd come to Brainard. Dewey had gone off on his own, got his own store, selling hardware and tools. But he wasn't a businessman like his father. Dewey was a salesman. He loved to talk, but he let things go, bills, inventory, expenses. He bought too much of all the wrong things, and there was never any money. He started drinking, and he went off on buying trips to Chicago almost once every month. He said they were buying trips, but he met a woman there. I found letters in his desk. Maybe I shouldn't have looked, but I did. He thought he was in love with her, just like he was with me in Alsace. I think Dewey would have loved any woman who would give herself to him. He was afraid he would break her heart. I felt sorry for Dewey, but I had given up on him as a man. I took over the business. His father gave me lots of advice, and I made a good business of it. I loved his father so much. He was what Dewey would have been if Dewey had ever grown up.

IT WAS WHEN DEWEY was on one of those trips to Chicago. Mr. Brande knew what was happening. We never spoke of it, but I think he felt responsible for Dewey and wanted to make it up to me. Madame Schumann-Heink was giving a special last concert in Grand Rapids. He took me down on the train, and we got rooms at the Pantlind Hotel. It was perfectly respectable. I was his daughter-in-law. I hadn't heard German sung in so long, and I'd been to the opera only once as a girl, in Strasbourg. The concert was thrilling, and we had a late supper in the hotel. We drank almost two bottles of Rhine wine in the spirit of that night, and we danced. He was so courtly, and I felt more like a woman than I ever had with Dewey.

He saw me back to my room. We were both a little tipsy, but we knew what we were doing. At the door to my room, he took hold of both my hands. He held me to look at me in my long dress, and he said to me, "Lorraine," and he sighed when he said it. His manner said so much more than his words, and I put my arms around his neck and drew him to me. I wanted him to feel my breasts against him, and I kissed him as no daughter would kiss him, and he gave himself to me in that moment. I pulled his head to my bare shoulders. He kissed me there, and then I felt him remember himself. He pulled back and held me by the hands as he had before, and he said my name again. He knew then that I loved him, and that was enough for both of us. It was something we shared until he died.

DEWEY AND I BOTH MARRIED AGAIN, and had the children we never had together. I had never been able to get pregnant with Dewey, and he blamed me for that. Then, after the woman in Chicago, we stopped trying. Dewey married Lucille Parker. He stopped his drinking and went to work in her father's wholesale grocery. Lucille died giving birth to their third son, Roy, and my husband, Darrell Stroven, drowned on a fishing trip to Canada.

IT'S FUNNY TO ME NOW after all these years. Dewey and I are having the courtship we never had because of the war. It's fun, and it's also a little bit silly, but Dewey doesn't see that. He's convinced he's in love with me. He sends me notes across the hall with the nurses. He sent me flowers on my last birthday, and I pretended to be thrilled. It's harmless. The nurses wheel us down to the TV room, and we play checkers. Yesterday he looked at me across the board, the first time I think he ever caught on that I had been letting him win, and he gave me that big sad-eyed smile that has come to him with age. He said, "Lorraine," very softly, and I thought my heart was going to stop. I saw his father there for a moment, as he was that night

66

in 1929 in the Pantlind Hotel, and I loved him for that. I think I might even have blushed. I'm sure Dewey thought I was blushing for him. Well, let him. At our age, what's the difference? I've learned that much about life. We can think what we want to think.

"Shall we play again, Lorraine?" he asks me.

CONVERSATION

A cloud moved over the street, and then the sun shone on the window again as instantly as if someone had switched on a light. I looked at my empty hand hanging over the edge of the bed and had the sensation of my father's hand still in mine, his fingers moving over my knuckles in laughter and explanation. It wasn't a happy dream, but in it I was having a conversation. I don't think I've really had a conversation with anyone since my father died.

I read books. I've always read books, and I work at the library. People write messages to me, and I point at things and write messages to them, but it's not like it was with my father. Holding my hands and tapping my knuckles with his fingers, he could tell me anything, and I could tell him whatever I felt. I've never been able to read lips or to develop a sign language with anyone else. I know they have that now. I see people on television in a little box in the lower left-hand corner of the screen. They wave their hands around like they are making shadow pictures, but it doesn't mean anything to me. When I was growing up they would point to a word on a page and move their lips and say, "cow." I'd get that it was "cow," but when they would try to tell me something, it looked like "ow" to me.

"Write it," I'd write on my pad. I used to be able to talk, too, or I thought I could. But I could tell by people's faces that it didn't sound like real talk. Sometimes they'd pretend to understand, or they'd stifle a look of amusement that said, "What the hell is this?" It was like being in a box with all kinds of false doors. You could open them and step through sometimes, but you'd find yourself right back in the box.

In school I'd be given books and a desk in a corner of the room. I'd read the books they gave me and lots of other ones too, and I'd pass the tests, so they left me pretty much alone. I know a lot about books. I take care of the card catalogue at the library. I put the returns back where they belong on the shelves, and I can help people find things if they'll write what they want on my pad.

More than anything, I want to go fishing again with my dad. We could sit all day and watch our lines piercing the dark surface of the water. We could hold hands and talk about the weather and the sky and the music box from before the meningitis. I remember the music box; I almost remember the tune. At least I can remember what a tune is, how music makes a person feel. Then there were headaches and vomiting and being in bed a long time, and that's all I know about sound.

I GOT UP AND LOOKED out the window. The men from Wheeler Electric were crossing Main Street on their way into the Dinner Bell for breakfast. I used to go in there every morning, up until about a month ago. I know those guys. They sit at the big round table at the back with Dale McBride, the plumber, and Bob DeGeest from the Chevy garage. I went to school with Bob. We'd nod and wave to each other when I'd come in. I knew all those guys. And I'd sit at the table up near the front. People feel uncomfortable if I sit down with them. They feel they have to talk, and they end up getting red and asking for the check before they've even finished their second cup of coffee.

From that table, I could look across the street and see the window of my apartment above the hardware store. I could read the paper and I could point to whatever I wanted on the menu. Maude, the owner, was always sweet to me. I'm not a bad looking guy really. She'd squeeze my cheek or my hand and touch my hair when she would first come over to my table with a pot of coffee. She knew my dad. She used to go out with him after my mother died. Sometimes I'd ride in the back of the car, and we'd go to the movies in Muskegon. Maude could tell my dad what to tell me, and I'd tell him, with my hand, what to say to her. Once I told him to tell her I loved her, and I felt like I was going to pop right out of my skin. She blushed, and then she kissed me. Then Sandy came to work at the Dinner Bell. Sandy was a good name for her. She had sandy blonde hair and blue eyes. Maude introduced us her first day at work. She put her hand on my face when she told Sandy about me, and I kissed her hand before she took it away. I blushed, and Maude blushed as she had that night in the car, and Sandy smiled and winked at me.

I think Sandy had worked as a waitress before. I used to watch her, and she was good. She would've been good at anything. She had so much self-confidence about her. That's what I was watching really. She looked like she knew everything, and she laughed a lot. I watched her once in her back yard with her dog. I was walking down Elm Street on my day off, and she was teaching her dog tricks. It was a big black dog, a retriever of some kind maybe; it looked as big as a bear. She was making it jump. She had set up a series of jumps around the yard, and when she waved her hand in the air, the dog would run around the inside of the fence, taking one jump after another, and when it had taken them all, it would come skidding to a stop at her feet and sit there as if to say, "What's next?"

After Maude introduced us, Sandy was sweet to me too. Sometimes she'd touch my shoulder when she came over to take my order. It was after I met Sandy, more than any time since my father died, that I wished I could talk. Around her I felt bottled up, like there was so much inside me that had to come out right now, but it just dribbled out in winks and smiles. One time I took her hand in mine before she could take it away from my shoulder. She looked at me for a minute and I felt so much in that look. After that, I'd take her hand every once in a while, and she never tried to pull it away.

Then one day about a month ago, she brought me a note along with my check. The note said, "Would you like to go swimming with me tomorrow afternoon?" I was supposed to work the next day at the library, but I nodded yes right away. Sandy smiled as if she was really pleased, and she sat down at my table for a minute. She turned over the paper with the note on it, and she wrote, "I'll make a picnic. I'll pick you up at noon. Where?"

"At the library," I wrote under her question.

She squeezed my arm and then got up and took coffee over

to a table of guys I didn't know. They were wearing suits and must've been from out of town, salesmen calling on Clark's maybe. She handled them so easily. They were flirting with her I think, but she was going to go out with me. I felt all warm inside, wrapped around the secret those men at the table didn't know. I could tell they liked Sandy by the way they got red when they smiled. She said something that made them all laugh, and then for a minute they avoided looking at each other. That's my Sandy, I thought. I think she put them in their place. She was sweet about it, and she did it in stride.

I asked Mr. Medgars for the afternoon off, and he nodded yes. He said, "Sure," as if he was pleased. I never take any time off, and I think he was happy I asked. Mr. Medgars was a friend of my father's, and he took me on at the library when I got out of high school. I love the library. I belong there. It's like I have conversations with the authors of the books. They speak so clearly, and when someone wants something, I know right where it is. It's kind of like I'm introducing them.

"Where are you going?" Mr. Medgars wrote down on my pad.

"I've got a date," I wrote. I felt a little funny writing that, and I felt proud. "We're going on a picnic."

"Wonderful!" Mr. Medgars wrote. He looked pleased. You might even say he looked thrilled. He had been a good friend of my dad's, and it made him happy. I'd never had a date before.

That night I spent a lot of time in front of the mirror in my bedroom, wondering how I must look to Sandy. I looked at my face and tried to make it say things I might want to tell her. I tried to think messages through my eyes. I practiced moving my lips. I watched my mouth open, watched my tongue push off and fall away, watched my lips purse, almost as if to make a kiss, watched the lower one flick against my front teeth. I practiced again and again, and I forced air up out of my throat. I kept doing it in bed, and I kept waking up and looking at the clock all night long.

IT WAS SANDY'S DAY OFF, and Maude brought me coffee. I wanted to tell her about my date, and then felt a little afraid of spoiling it by telling people. Maybe they would look at me funny. Maybe they would laugh. I figured Maude probably knew anyway.

I took my swimsuit to work with me and kept it in my desk drawer until Sandy picked me up at noon. "My uncle's got a place on the lake," she wrote, and she squeezed my hand. She turned on the radio as we drove out of town. I put my hand on the speaker and nodded my head to the vibrations so she'd know I knew what kind of music she was listening to. She laughed and smiled as if to say, "Yes, that's it. You've got it."

We turned off the highway and drove a long way through the woods before we came to a cabin on the water. It was a beautiful little lake, a lot like I imagined Walden Pond must have been when Thoreau lived there, and there were no other houses around. Sandy showed me into a bedroom in the cabin and pointed to my swimming suit.

When I came out, I saw Sandy just pulling her suit up around her knees. She was facing away from me and didn't seem at all bothered, when she turned around, that I had seen her naked. I don't think anything bothered Sandy. I thought of the dog

73

going over the jumps and the salesmen at the table. She took my hand and led me out onto the dock. She dove into the water, and when she came up, her hair clung to her head, smooth and shiny, like the coat of an otter. She beckoned to me, and I dove in after her. The water was dark and clear, and as I got deeper, it got colder. I stayed under for a moment and looked at her legs. Under the water, I almost thought I could hear. Maybe it was the water rushing around my head in my dive, or maybe it was that underwater Sandy would be deaf too. We dove down again and again and looked at each other and blew bubbles. She put her arms around my neck and hugged me, and I hugged her back. It felt funny to be hugging a girl in the water.

We climbed out on the dock and lay there a minute in the sun. But then the deer flies began biting, and so she took my hand and led me to the cabin. We dried off and she laid the picnic out on the table on the porch. I ate half a chicken sandwich, and Sandy opened a couple of beers.

After lunch, Sandy opened two more beers, and then she took me by the hand and led me to a big lounge. I sat down on the lounge, and Sandy stood in front of me and peeled her bathing suit down as easily as if she were just stepping out of her shoes. I couldn't believe it was happening. She was so beautiful without any clothes on, as beautiful as the girls in the magazines, and she had a little mole or birthmark on her belly, just beside her navel. She took me by the hand and made me stand up, and she pulled my suit down too. I don't need to say what else happened then exactly, but it was everything I'd ever imagined, and more. It was like a conversation, only more than anything that anyone could say. And Sandy laughed a lot. I could feel the convulsions of her body. I could feel the vibrations of her throat.

After we got dressed, we sat at the table on the porch, and she opened two more beers. I held up my beer can to touch it to hers the way I'd seen people do, but she didn't get what I was doing, and she just smiled at me. It was different than the way she'd smiled at me before. It was like she was thinking about something else while she was smiling, as if she might have been saying, "That's nice." I thought maybe this was the time for it, something to bring her back to me. I ran it by once in my head, and then I took her hand across the table, and I squeezed it. She was sitting there with her beer in her other hand, staring out over the lake, and she turned to look at me. I lifted her hand up, and I kissed her fingers, and then I opened my mouth and I said, "I love you." I said it as clearly and carefully as I'd practiced it in front of the mirror.

Sandy's face went slack. Her mouth fell open, and I knew right away it had been the wrong thing to do. Her eyes got wide and she started to laugh way back in her throat. Then she laughed harder and she wrapped her arms around her sides. She shook her head, and it looked like she was trying to catch her breath. She wiped the tears away from her eyes, and then she reached across the table and patted my hand and smiled again.

IN THE DREAM, I FOUND my father in a room filled with fishing rods. It was like a store full of rods for sale or rent, and it was on a dock. It was a beautiful morning with a light breeze, and more than anything in the world, I wanted him to go fishing with me. He sat there in his brown fedora, and he took hold of my hand, and he laughed. It was that kind of laugh he had, all inside himself like a wave sucking back in before it breaks. "There are all kinds of reasons," his fingers said, "but they don't matter. This is silly." He shifted around in his chair as if to say, let's be serious, and he said, "Look, I've been dead for ten years now. I can't go fishing with you. You can't go fishing with dead people."

"Ya, but," I said, but my fingers moved against nothing. I fixed myself a cup of instant coffee, and I sat by the window till the guys from Wheeler Electric came back out of the Dinner Bell and got in their truck and drove away. Pretty soon I'll get dressed and go down to Fred's Fine Foods. I don't know many people there, but they'll get to know me. The food's at least as good as at the Dinner Bell, and the hashbrowns are better, crispier.

We're stocking the new children's room at the library now. They're only children's books, but they've got to be catalogued just like *War and Peace*. The other day Mr. Medgars told me he had been librarian there for thirty-eight years, and he's never had anyone do a better job than I do.

GRASS FIRES

It was a family affair, that's all you could say for it. Floyd Pekel crashed his S-10 pickup right through the front door of his cousin Randall Bingham's funeral home, and everybody was talking about it down at the Dinner Bell. "Well, it was convenient," Maude Troupe said, as she poured coffee. I'll bet I heard her say it five times that morning as people came in. "Did you hear about Floyd Pekel?" And then the story, and then the comment about its being convenient. Maude doesn't really feel that way. She cared about Floyd—he was one of the regulars—but it's the kind of amusement we get around here. It makes a day memorable. I'm sure it was a memorable day for Floyd's family and Randy's too.

There was no need for an ambulance. Floyd was dead, and he was already in a funeral home. You can imagine what a shock it must have been for Randy. He was down in the basement embalming Mrs. VanSant when it happened. I used to work for Randy, and Mike Traxler, who works for him now, told me about it. They were pumping the fluid into Mrs. VanSant when all hell broke loose. "I thought it was an earthquake or I don't know what," Mike said. "Plaster powdered the air like smoke," he said. "And then it was quiet, and then there was another crash when one of the big columns outside let loose and crashed through the front room. That was when the light over the embalming table came down, and it all went dark."

He and Randy felt their way upstairs, thinking maybe it was World War III. And then when they saw the red fender of the pickup and that flashing red light, that was it. Everybody knows Floyd's truck. "Oh my God," Randy said. Mike said he said that about five times. He said it when the lights went out. He said it when he recognized Floyd's truck and again when he checked out Floyd and saw he was dead. He called the hospital anyway, probably because of what happened three summers ago when I was working for him.

Back then we drove the ambulance for the hospital too. It was contracted out, and we won the bid. Later they changed the rules because people felt kind of funny about being taken to the hospital in an ambulance that doubled as a hearse. They felt it was a conflict of interest, thought we'd just as soon bring 'em to the home as take 'em to the hospital. It wasn't that way though. Enough people die every day. We didn't need to promote the business. A lot of people think funeral directors are some kind of ghouls, but they're not. I've known several of them, and I worked for Randy, and it's no easy life. You're dealing with sadness all the time and trying to be a comfort to people. It's an odd kind of calling, but that's what it is.

Well, this day three years ago we got a call about 6:00 a.m.— an accident down at the west end of town. This guy was drunk, I'm quite sure, and he'd run down Main Street about eighty miles an hour and crashed into a telephone pole right in front of the Mini Mart. He'd broken the telephone pole right off like a matchstick and sat slumped in his smashed-up Mustang convertible like a half-empty bag of barley. Ed Twing, the coroner, was already there, and he'd pronounced the guy dead. That was in July; the sun had just barely broken over Main Street, and already it was hot. It seemed like the dead man was steaming. I didn't know him. He lived up near Hesperia and worked at Continental. So Doc Twing said he was dead, and we wheeled out the stretcher. Randy reached in over the back of the seat, under the guy's arms, locked his wrists around the dead man's ribs and yanked him out of the Mustang. Randy's pretty big. He made All-State Honorable Mention as tackle in high school. There's a plaque that says so; I used to see it every day in the gym. Randy's ten years older than me.

This guy was kind of stuck in there, and Randy had to yank two or three times to get him loose. We didn't think much about it at the time, but it sure was hot. We got him in the ambulance, took him to the home and pulled into the garage. We were barely awake. We'd both gotten called out of bed and decided we'd have some coffee before we started work on him. We didn't want to let him sit too long in that heat though. You'd be surprised how quick a body will start to spoil. So we had some coffee and a couple of cigarettes and talked about how loaded this guy must've been to be tearing down Main Street like that at 6:00 a.m. and to run straight off into a telephone pole. "He must have been determined," I remember Randy said, and I knew what he meant.

Well, then we figured we'd better get at it, so we went back to the garage, opened the back door of the ambulance, and here's this guy sitting up there on the stretcher holding a Lucky Strike in his hand, and he says, "Got a light?"

I don't know which was a bigger shock to Randy, that dead man asking for a light or his cousin Floyd dead in his S-10 pickup right there in the lobby. "Holy shit!" he said that time.

Later we figured it was probably Randy's yanking on him that brought him back to life, and Mike told me that after Randy called the hospital, he reached in the window of the pickup and tried the same thing on Floyd. He yanked and yanked, but it didn't do any good. That guy in the Mustang— Collins was his name—was back on the streets that same afternoon, but Floyd was gone for good. Doc Twing did an autopsy and said he was probably gone before he hit the front door; heart attack, massive infarction, he called it. Nothing to be done.

"Convenient," Maude Troup said, but that was just a joke. People have to talk about something, and that was something alright. The last time I saw Floyd was in the Dinner Bell when there was a grass fire. The red light on the dash of his pickup started flashing. Floyd was a volunteer fireman, and that flasher would set off automatically when the signal went out from the firehouse. I was sitting at the big round table with Floyd, talking about how dry it had been for April, and Maude had just brought him his soup. I worked on Floyd's farm last summer's haying. He was the boss, but I was the one had to keep prodding him on because he always wanted to stop and talk. He'd talk about things he'd read in books, about how all these big cathedrals in Europe were built in the same century and why do you suppose that was, or did a bird have a consciousness? Stuff like that, you couldn't answer. He'd go on like that till the hay'd be ruined in the field if you didn't get him going.

We were putting the second cutting up in the loft last August, and Floyd was going on about how nothing really existed, how you couldn't find out where any atom was and how fast it was moving at the same time. "You think this barn is real?" he said. "It's nothing but energy," and he slammed his fist against the doorjamb.

"Well, that fire's real," I said, looking over his shoulder. The fire was on the haywagon. It'd been loaded so heavy that all the way back to the barn one of the tires was rubbing on the metal plate in the wagon bed. We had it half unloaded, and it must've been smouldering all the time we were working on it. Then it burst into flame, matter turning into energy, just as Floyd was talking about it. There ya go, I thought. We both jumped from the loft, maybe fifteen feet down onto the wagon, and started pitching off bales as fast as we could. We only lost three of 'em to the fire, but I had to laugh about that. "Ya see?" Floyd said, "ya see?" He was happy about the fire once we got it put out.

Floyd was telling me how his son had been accepted at Michigan State and how he was going to become an educated man and then someday maybe come back and take over the farm, when Maude hollered, "Fire, Floyd! Your flasher's on." Floyd was up and gone without ever touching his soup, and not three minutes later he zipped past out front in the chemical truck heading west to the fire. They're used to that at the Dinner Bell, and they don't charge firemen for interrupted meals. It was Maude's homemade beef-noodle soup. I hadn't ordered yet, so I told Maude I'd take it. "Suits me," she said, and I was eating Floyd's soup when Floyd went by.

I THOUGHT ABOUT THAT at the funeral, about eating Floyd's soup. Convenient, Maude said, but the funeral had to be moved to the Leadly Funeral Home east of town. The Bingham Funeral Home was a wreck, and Randy was in no condition to carry it off, anyway. They had to move Mrs. VanSant's funeral to Leadly's, too, but I'm sure that the lost business was the last thing on Randy's mind.

Mike said that it looked like a disaster area when he and Randy climbed the stairs, that red light flashing all around the rubble of the room. It turned out Floyd was on his way to a fire when his heart let go.

It was a nice service. The preacher talked about how public-spirited Floyd was, how helping others was God's business and how that's what Floyd was about when he died. And I thought about Floyd being energy now, about that being the way he'd think about it. And I felt sad for the family. Floyd's wife, Eva, cried out loud when they carried the casket out, and his son won't be going to State now. Randy was one of the pallbearers, and he was crying too.

I'll think about Floyd every time I smell the smoke of grass fires.

I WENT DOWN to the Dinner Bell right after the interment. I sat at the round table with the mechanics from the Chevy garage on their coffee break, and I had a bowl of Maude's home-made beef-noodle soup. It was just a little saltier this time. Bob DeGeest said, "You must have a tapeworm. I seen you in here eating lunch." I just smiled though. Later that afternoon, the whistle blew again. There were seven more grass fires that spring.

HARDBALL

There's a new McDonald's there now, asphalt drive, manicured lawn, curb and gutter, nothing like it was then. There was poverty here and there in Brainard but nowhere as concentrated as it was at The Oaks. Living there, a person was part of a lower order, a separate species who, on summer evenings, escaped to the benches in the park. Oaks People, they were called, and they breathed in the cool night air, forgetting for a while the yellow brick walls and lightless windows, the tarpaper roofs and sagging front porches, the rusting appliances in the unkempt yard. We wondered about life at The Oaks, but nobody who didn't have to went in to find out.

In all the time I knew Craig Mosely, I never set foot in the place. We were poor, but my mother drew the line. "You go in there, you get labeled," she said. She'd let me have Craig over once in a while. She could see he was nice. But Craig never wanted me over to his place, so it never came up. He must have had a mother; I don't remember her at all. I remember his father though. A lot of people my age and older remember Claude Mosely. He was a big man who looked like he was made out of spare parts. Sometimes his shoes wouldn't match, and his hair was stiff and matted and stuck out from his head like the crown of a kingfisher. I remember coming out of the movies one winter night with my friend, Carol Slocum, seeing Claude Mosely staggering in front of Bob's Bar. "Money's no good," he said. He tore the change from his pockets and scattered it over the icy sidewalk. He pulled his pockets inside out and lurched toward the west end of Main. "God damn God!" He pounded on the locked doors of stores and restaurants. "God damn God!" he hollered again and again, his breath smoking in the bitter cold, his voice still frightening in the distance. Carol and I scrambled over the sidewalk and picked coins out of the ice and salt. A crumpled dollar bill had tumbled into the gutter. I smoothed it out and dried it against my skirt. We couldn't believe our good fortune. I didn't connect any of this with Craig. It wasn't till I told my mother the next day that she told me my friend Craig was Claude Mosely's son. I kept the money for a week and then gave it to Craig. It was almost two dollars, which was a lot to us then. Claude Mosely's son. I couldn't believe it.

When Craig grew up, people forgot about Claude. For a long time Craig was somebody in Brainard, our only professional athlete. "He used to be with the Tigers," everyone would say when they pointed him out to visitors. He had that fastball, and they brought him up from the Evansville farm club when Joe Sparma got hurt. He pitched five games for Detroit and won three of them. I remember Ernie Harwell's voice on the radio, "Craig Mosely, out of Brainard, Michigan, a hard thrower just up from Evansville. He's turned things around here for the

Bengals." Then he threw out his arm against the Red Sox, and they sent him back to Indiana for reconditioning. He spent seven years trying to get it back, to get back to the majors. Then they dropped him down to double A ball in Birmingham, and he gave it up. But he'd pitched in Tiger Stadium, and that was what everyone remembered.

WHEN HE CAME BACK to Brainard, The Oaks was gone, condemned and torn down. It was just a grassy lot on the corner of Gilbert and Main, and people had mostly forgotten. Craig was a local treasure. Everyone called him by name like they were all old friends, and more often than not, the first year or so, the meals and the drinks were free. They were anxious to have him seen at Fred's Fine Foods or Antonelli's. Almost every place in town had an autographed picture on the wall, the same one of Craig in his Tiger whites. But it wore off in time. At his funeral, when the minister said, "We don't judge a life by a single act," he meant Craig's suicide of course, but I thought of that first game in Tiger Stadium when he came out of nowhere to pitch a one-hitter against the Yankees, and Ernie Harwell was hoarse with excitement. "Craig Mosely. There's a name for the books. Eleven strike-outs his first game in the majors." He had his picture in *Sports Illustrated*, and for a couple of weeks there, Craig was a star. He had groupies wherever they went. "They used to lick my arms," he told me.

The coffin was closed, and I thought of his arms. I'd had a crush on Craig when we were kids. I guess I always did. But I could play ball, and that's how he thought of me. I guess none

86

of the guys really thought of me as a girl, once we got past playing doctor. I'm a big woman, and I was big then, and I could catch Craig's fastballs. Until we got to junior high, I was the only one brave enough. God, they'd come in there. Wham! You could hear the air behind them, hissing like a rocket, right at your face. Then, wham! You were on your toes, thrusting forward with the pitch so as not to get knocked on your butt. And wham! You just crouched down and held out the mitt like a target. That's all you could do. You just knew they'd come in there. It was like making love. I trusted Craig. I knew he wouldn't hurt me. I was the only girl they'd let play and the only one who wanted to. A lot of girls wanted Craig though. He was good-looking and quiet like Montgomery Clift, and when you saw him pitch, you felt all that power pent up inside. "Chuck it in here Craig baby, right here baby. Burn it to me," I'd say. Stuff like that. I was his glove. I called the pitches between my legs.

Baseball was everything for Craig, and when he pitched that first no-hitter his sophomore year, it didn't matter about The Oaks. We won the State two years running, and the Chamber of Commerce put up a sign:

WELCOME TO BRAINARD
Pop. 4,262
State Class B Baseball Champs
1960
1961

Kenny Blondene was catching for him then, and he was good too, but I was there for every pitch. I felt every one that came through, and I hurt with those few that got hit. He pitched three no-hitters his junior year, and the scouts were showing up.

I LOOKED AROUND THE CHURCH, and I wanted to puke. All those hypocrites showing up now he was dead. A week ago they wouldn't have given him the dust off their shoes. Five years after he came back to Brainard, he was nobody. They'd made a hero out of him, and he couldn't live up to it. Nobody could. They took his picture down when they remodeled at Fred's and it never went back up. Craig had started drinking, and when they said, "He used to pitch for the Tigers," it was like they were saying, "Can you believe it?" He tried insurance. He tried used cars. He got along on his name for a while, but it wasn't baseball. He ended up working production at Clark's, and the people couldn't stand it. They wouldn't leave him alone, and he got in fights. They talked about his dad again. Finally I stood up in the middle of the eulogy. "You assholes," I shouted. "You didn't know Craig Mosely. You didn't even like him." I was shaking, and nobody looked around. They just hunched in their pews, trying to pull their heads in like turtles. They wanted to pretend it wasn't happening, that I wasn't there to show them what they were. But I didn't really stand up and shout. I just thought about it, and I felt prickly all over.

I NEVER DID MARRY. I never got asked. I play softball, slow-pitch, for Gilbert Chevrolet. We win it all, and I bowl. I sweep the halls at the high school, a custodial engineer they call me. I never cared about any man but Craig, and he never thought of

88

me as a woman, but that one time. It was two years ago, a warm night in April, he came to my trailer. We were buddies. He respected me as an athlete. He'd been drinking, really drinking. His face was all cut up, and he wasn't so cute anymore. There'd been trouble at Antonelli's. From what I could make out, Joe Antonelli and his two sons had pitched him out on the street. It had happened before. There were all different kinds of stories. His eye was cut and his lip, and one of his lower teeth was gone. "The Lasagna brothers jumped me," is what he said. His words were slurred, and his eyes never quite looked at any one thing. I got a wet rag, and I cleaned him up. "I feel sorry for old man Antonelli," he blubbered out. "He's gonna have to get hurt."

I put some iodine on his cut, and he started to cry. I got him out of his clothes. I put him to bed, and I crawled in with him and held him in my arms. I knew Craig Mosely, before the scouts came, before Evansville. He went on crying and I held him to my breast. His body jerked with sobs. "It's all gone. It's all gone," he cried again and again. I put my hand in his hair and held him to me, and I felt him drift off to sleep. I felt those muscles in his shoulders. I could feel that power still, and I held him all night long.

In the morning I felt him stir. I woke up, and he was making love to me. He was kissing my neck and my breasts, and I let him. He climbed on top of me, and I let him. I was forty years old, and I'd never been with a man, I mean really, since maybe I was thirteen. I thought about catching for him again. For a few minutes he was pitching to me again. I thought about those groupies licking his arms.

And then it was over, just like that. It was like he was just waking up. He rolled out of bed and went into the bathroom. I made him some coffee, and he got dressed and left. He thanked me, and it was just like we were buddies again. I didn't know what to think. But for a while there, there was something. I don't know. I felt young again, and Craig was young, with his good fastball and all that promise.

NEW PEOPLE

For a minute I was in love with her, and then she was gone.
Sometimes it doesn't take more than a glance. I've had that
happen in airports, on the street or in libraries. You see a
woman, your eyes meet for just an instant longer than you can
ascribe to chance, and she stays with you for years, maybe for-
ever.

I was driving into town, and we passed each other on the
angle-bend at the bottom of the valley on Wilcox. You can see
an oncoming car there as soon as you crest the hill from the
north, see it half a mile from where it comes out of the woods,
and you wonder if you'll meet at the bend or if maybe you'll get
through it first. It's kind of a silly game I play with myself, as
I would avoid stepping on cracks when I was a child or would
consider it a good omen if I had gotten safely across Main
Street on my way home from school before the four o'clock
whistle blew at Clark's.

I'd been watching her car all the way, a white Ford, and as we
got to the bend, I saw her face, and she was looking at me. For
just that moment her face stood out larger and brighter than
anything around it; the car, the rain-puddled road, the new
grass along the shoulders, all shrank away. There was only her

face and those black eyes looking at me as if I were someone she'd been searching for and had just spotted in a crowd. The moment lasted a little longer than it took our cars to pass. I glanced in the rearview mirror to see her splash into the puddle I had just come through. I saw the cat dart across the road, saw her rear tires skidding as she swerved. And then the willows on the inside of the bend came between us, and I was busy getting my car stopped, the front end pulling to the right on the wet asphalt.

Her car was upended in the drainage ditch and already filling with water. There were things floating around inside of it, books, underwear, towels. A beautiful white blouse with bouffant sleeves lay on the water inside the window. I stumbled into the ditch by the driver's door, but I couldn't get her out. She lay slumped over the wheel, and I couldn't get the door open. I pulled on the handle and pounded on the window, trying to break the glass, and I watched the water ride up and lift the shiny black hair from her neck. Rex Vleem said I was crying when he got there, that I was sitting on the bank with my legs in the water, crying, but I don't remember it. I remember the police cars arriving and the ambulance. I remember someone leading me away and wrapping a blanket around me. Then they took me to the hospital and kept me there for an hour or two. They said I'd been in shock.

Somebody brought my car. It was parked in the lot across the street from the emergency room. The woman was dead, and there was no one I could talk to. The police had questioned me. I'd told them what I'd seen happen, but I didn't tell them about her eyes. I wanted to talk about her eyes. I felt as if someone I loved had died and there was no one I could talk to. I drove home and took a hot shower and put on clean clothes. Forry Traveer was there by the bend with his wrecker, pulling the car from the ditch when I went by. I only glanced and then drove on up the hill.

Lynn Stroud; that was her name. I called Kenny Brooks, the Chief of Police, and he told me. He gave me her address on Linden Street. Kenny and I were in school together. I see him at Lions' Club, and sometimes we'll stop in at the Moose for a beer. He asked me how I was doing, and I said fine. But the truth is I didn't know.

I went over to her house on Linden. I hadn't thought of a reason; I just knew I had to go. "I'm Andy Cooper," I told the man who came to the door. "I saw the accident."

At first I didn't realize how young he was. If someone is past puberty and doesn't have white hair, I assume they're about my age. "Please come in," he said. "I'm Gary Stroud."

The house had an unsettled look, no pictures on the walls, no books on the shelves. There were a few other people there, milling about uncomfortably, a few faces I recognized but couldn't put together with names, people from Clark's, the apple juice company. It turned out the Strouds had just moved to Brainard. He'd taken a job with Clark's and had started work only the week before.

"I understand you tried to save her," Gary Stroud said. He seemed quite calm, maybe subdued was the word.

"I couldn't do anything," I said. "I'm sorry."

"They told me you did everything you could," he said. "Would you like a drink?"

I don't drink much, but right then I knew I wanted something. He fixed me a whiskey and water and I took several good swallows of it right away.

"This is a nice town," he said. "I'm glad you came over."

"You just moved here, didn't you?" It went on like that. He told me they'd come down from Traverse City. He was an agricultural engineer, originally from Steubenville, Ohio. He'd been with a big orchard up in Grand Traverse County and had been hired by Clark's as their chief produce man. "I don't know any of these people very well." He nodded toward the other men, all congregated in the far corner of the living room. "These things are pretty awkward. Nobody knows what to do, but everyone wants to do something."

"I guess that includes me," I said. "I lost my wife a year ago. I always thought I'd just want to be by myself when that happened, but it helped having people around."

"I'm sorry about your wife," he said.

"It was almost a relief when it happened," I told him. "Leukemia. I couldn't bear the suffering anymore, seeing her waste away with that fierce look of pain in her eyes. I wanted her to die and get it over with, but at the same time I didn't want to let her go. We'd been married for twenty-five years."

He listened attentively, his wide, calm eyes taking in everything I said, and suddenly I was deeply embarrassed. "Excuse me," I said. "I came here because you've just lost your wife, and now I'm going on about myself."

"No, please." He put his hand on my elbow. "This has been

hard for you, I know. The police told me about it, what you tried to do. I'd like to talk with you, maybe later, after things settle down. The families are coming in tonight. I'd appreciate it if you'd come see me when they've gone. Please."

"I understand," I said, and we shook hands. But I didn't understand, really.

I went to the funeral because I wanted to. I couldn't forget those eyes I'd seen for only an instant. I'd never known her. I'd watched her die, and yet I couldn't believe she was dead. I can believe Marcie's dead. I'd seen it coming for so long; I suffered her loss long before she died. But this woman, or girl, Lynn Stroud. I'd never heard her voice, never seen her walk across a room, and yet I just couldn't believe she was no longer on this earth.

I didn't go to Gary's after the service. I went home, and I walked around in my empty house. It was almost May, and I had eighty acres still to plant in strips of wheat and corn, but I didn't have any heart for it that afternoon. I made myself a cup of instant, and I sat at the kitchen table. I could hear robins in the trees around the house, the rasping of red-wing blackbirds and the coo of a mourning dove.

I called my son in East Lansing, but he wasn't home. I called my daughter at Western, and we talked for ten minutes. She told me about getting ready for finals, how she felt she was prepared, how some of the girls were taking pills to stay up all night and study, and how she had a job at K-Mart there that she thought she'd take for the summer. I wanted to tell her about Lynn Stroud, but what could I say? I told her a woman had been killed on Wilcox, at the big bend by the marsh, and we agreed it was a dangerous stretch of road. I told her I loved her and wished her luck with her exams.

I got to planting the next day and got all but ten acres of corn in that week before the fuel pump went out on the Farmall. Sunday I went over to Montcalm County to watch the annual Plow Day, where the Friends of Draft Horses bring their teams to plow forty acres the old way. I called Gary Stroud when I got home that night, and he said he was doing okay. He said he was glad everyone had gone, that he was tired of condolences and that he wanted me to come over for dinner Monday night. I offered to take him out to the Highway Inn for burritos, but he said he'd rather I just come over. "How about six o'clock?" he said, and I said okay.

IT'S STRANGE HOW YOU go to seek comfort sometimes from the very people you should be comforting. Before I came back to the farm, I got my master's in history and taught three years at Michigan. I brought Marcie back to the farm for the first time to be with my mother, the summer after my father died. I'd had a falling out with my father years earlier. He was hurt and angry that I didn't want to carry on with the farm. He'd built up one of the finest dairy herds in the county, and he was haunted by the thought of its being auctioned off after he was gone. I never liked farming and dreamed only of escaping a life among cows. My mother had come down to our wedding in Detroit, but as far as my father was concerned, he had no son. Not taking on the farm might have been bad enough, but being a teacher had compounded it. "Useless as tits on a boar," he'd said when I first expressed my interest to him. "Parasites." In his mind, if you didn't add to the GNP, you didn't count. My mother had been proud of me, but she wouldn't stand up to my father.

So we came back that spring. We planned to be with her over the summer, to get her affairs in order, and I would keep the farm going until we could find someone else to manage it, but we never did. I sold off the herd after Mother died—I still don't care for cows—and turned the acres into cash crops. I found a new freedom in it, a joy I'd seldom known growing up, when everything was a chore I didn't want to do but had to get done.

So ostensibly we'd come back to help and comfort my mother, but we discovered that what was more important to us was her forgiveness. I think it was more important to Marcie than it was for me. She'd lost her parents years earlier and felt somehow she'd been to blame for separating me from mine. She wanted to know all about my father, and she and my mother would sit up late, sometimes long after I had gone to bed, and talk about old times.

Marcie grew stronger that summer, became a woman I loved so much more deeply than the girl I had married. And the change I'd seen come about in her through my mother's nurturing was, I think now, the biggest factor in my decision to stay.

That had happened almost twenty-five years before, and I thought back on it driving over to Gary's. I might tell myself it was just the thing to do, to be with someone in their loss, but that wasn't it really. I wanted some link, something to buffer the still clear image of that face I'd seen for only an instant.

GARY AND I HAD A FEW BEERS and talked about how there hadn't been any late frosts and how, if this weather continued, it looked like a bumper year for apples. I asked him how he liked Brainard so far and then felt it'd been a foolish question. "I'm sorry," I said. "You've hardly been here a week and under pretty unpleasant circumstances. I'm sure you haven't thought much about it either way."

"No, that's okay." He seemed a little amused by my apology. "I like the people at Clark's, and I know I'm going to like the job. I'd rather be buying apples than growing them."

We had chicken casserole for dinner. It wasn't bad. I guess it was part of the largess that comes with a funeral. People bring gifts of food on the theory that the survivors will be too grief-stricken to cook and have to be reminded that life has to go on. But Gary didn't seem grief-stricken, any more than he had when I'd seen him the day of the accident. We talked about the remarkable season the Tigers were having, the best twenty-eight game opening record in the history of baseball. We talked about Steubenville, Ohio, where he'd grown up. We talked about Brainard, and we talked about the Democratic primaries, everything but what I wanted to talk about. We had a few glasses of wine with dinner, and when our conversation lulled in our shared lack of enthusiasm for any of the presidential candidates, I said, "You seem to be handling this pretty well. Lynn's death, I mean." It seemed awkward, using her name as if I'd known her.

"You've been through it." He seemed quite philosophical. I figured it was at least partly the wine.

"I have," I nodded, "but mine was different. There was so much time to prepare."

Gary raised his eyebrows and stretched, the way I might stretch before getting up to speak at a township meeting. "It's not so different," he said.

"I don't understand. You certainly couldn't have been expecting it."

"Not in that way." He leaned back in his chair and looked up toward the ceiling. As the evening faded, it had gotten quite dark in the room. "I hadn't expected her death, but I was prepared for the loss."

"I don't get it. Excuse me . . ."

"No, that's okay. I want to explain. I haven't been able to talk about it, and I want to. I can talk to you because I didn't know you before. You probably noticed that her car was pretty well loaded with stuff."

I remembered the books and the clothes, the rack of blouses and dresses billowing in the water against the window. "Yes," I nodded. I hadn't thought of that again until he mentioned it.

"Well, she was leaving."

"Leaving?"

"Going back to Traverse City. Leaving me. I didn't really come here just because of the job. I thought we could start new in a new place."

"Something happened in Traverse City?"

"She met someone. It'd been going on for a year, and I hadn't seen it, hadn't even suspected. I was pretty wrapped up in my work. Lynn was a nurse at the medical center. She was dedicated to it. I thought we were happy; we'd been together since high school. There'd never been anyone else for either one of us. Then she broke down one night and told me about it. She said she couldn't stand it anymore, she said she didn't want to hurt me, but she didn't want to hurt him either. He was a doctor, and she saw him every day. I thought if we got away she'd be able to put it behind her. But it wasn't that way."

"So you came here?" I thought of her eyes, of the pleading expression in that one glimpse of her before the cat darted out of the willows.

"I'd had the job offer weeks before, and the night she told me all this, I decided to take it."

"And she agreed?"

"She agreed that night, I think mostly because she felt guilty. But she was so miserable she could hardly talk. I was a month finishing my work up there, and then three days after we got here, she told me she was leaving. I begged her to give it more time. She agonized over that, but I knew there wasn't any point in it. Then last Wednesday she packed up the car. It was raining, and I offered to help her, but she said no thanks. She was going back to Traverse City, going back to him, and she said she'd write. That was the real loss, and I'd seen it coming. That's why I wanted to talk to you and why I couldn't talk to her family or mine or anyone who knew us. What's the point? Why muddy the water? Let them think I'm grieving over her death. That wouldn't have been her choice."

It was night now; through the window, a beam from a street light lit one wall of the dining room and a strip of carpet behind his chair. "I understand," I said. I thought of her eyes again, but I couldn't picture her face.

"It's a terrible thing to say, but it's easier this way. I didn't wish her dead. I wish it hadn't happened. But it's easier than imagining her with someone else."

I SEE GARY ONCE IN A WHILE, see him on the street, and sometimes we'll stop for coffee. He likes his job, likes Brainard. But we never talk about Lynn. I think about her sometimes, and I think about Marcie. And I wonder what happens to those people we love who are gone.

I had an offer on the farm this spring. The offer came from Clark's, and it was quite a good price. They're thinking about growing some of their own apples for processing. My land is good high ground with ditches and a pond to draw off late frosts. I thought about it for a few days, but I decided I like farming. I don't know what else I would do.

SHARON

When Sharon told me she was going to file for a divorce, I said, "About time." I said, "Do it." I don't usually give advice in situations like that; I just listen. I figure it's up to the people to figure out what to do with their own lives, but with Sharon and Dale it's different. Some men are just misunderstood. At least you can say that about them and sometimes believe it. You can say they're depressed, they're trying to find themselves. Sometimes you just don't know.

When we were in high school and Dale first asked her out, Sharon thought she'd died and gone to heaven. "I just can't believe it, Sarah. Why me?" She'd dreamed about Dale since the sixth grade in the way you dream about movie stars, not expecting anything to come of it. Sharon was pretty, don't misunderstand, but she wasn't a cheerleader or anything, wasn't someone who might be on the Homecoming court. She was a farm girl and a good student, always on the honor roll, but she was quiet. She was the kind of girl you'd have to go back to look up in the yearbook ten years later to remember who she was.

Dale had a smile you might expect to see on daytime TV. He was on the Student Council because everyone liked him, and he also had the air of being a little bit bad. He had a '68 Chevy

convertible with quadraphonic stereo, and when Sharon asked
me why he'd asked her out, all I could say quite honestly was,
"I don't know." I thought maybe he was just playing with her.
Dale could've had just about any girl who wasn't going with
somebody and probably could've had some of the ones that
were. His name was in the papers every week during football
and basketball.

Sharon's parents weren't too keen on the idea at first. They
figured her to take a business course, be a secretary for a couple
of years, marry somebody solid like Ken Boonstra, have children, and be just like her mother. To Sharon's family, the important thing seemed to be just not making trouble. They were
the kind of people who would think of themselves as "good
Christian men and women" and would say so, just like that.

Well, two weeks after their first date, Dale and Sharon had
become a couple. It happens like that around here. You go out
with someone twice, and nobody else even thinks of asking
you. There was a lot of talk about it. "Can you believe it?"
Everyone was saying that and slapping their foreheads like
they'd seen snow in July. Maybe Dale thought she'd be easy.
Maybe, for him, she was. Or maybe he liked her because she
wasn't easy. She might've been the only one. Sharon wasn't by
any means what you'd call loose, but back then, with Dale Eggers, I might've been loose myself.

It's funny when I think of it, but when she'd been going out
with Dale for a while Sharon dressed sharper. I'm sure Dale
told her what to wear. She got her hair curled under. I think she
even lightened it. It wasn't really that Sharon changed so much
as it was that she became popular. I think that, after a few

months, if she'd broken up with Dale a lot of guys might've been interested in her. But it didn't happen. They were going steady, and by Christmas vacation nobody even talked about it being strange anymore. Dale was real busy with sports, and he worked weekends at the Shell station. Maybe he wanted a girl he could trust, one who wouldn't be making eyes over his shoulder.

The week after graduation I got a job at Antonelli's, the only restaurant in town with a liquor license. Sometimes people get rowdy, but the tips are bigger. My second night there, Sharon and Dale came in and told me they were engaged. I wanted to say, don't do it, but what would be the point? My parents got married right out of high school. My sister Noreen was on the way. But nobody listens to advice like that, so I screamed and hugged her and got real excited.

Dale got a job at the Chevy garage. He'd always been good with cars, and that was about all he wanted to do. He started going to church with Sharon, and her folks sort of decided he was okay. They got married in August, got a mobile home in the park across from the apple juice plant, and that was the beginning of the end of it as far as I could see.

I was the maid of honor, and Sharon was so excited she cried the night before the wedding. "Mrs. Dale Eggers." She just couldn't believe it. She shivered, and the tears made her mascara run. She never wore it before they got engaged. I'm sure that was Dale's doing too. Two months later she was crying on my shoulder, the day after the first night Dale forgot to come home.

He'd been drinking, she said. He'd had too much and slept

it off at Marv Stephens'. Things weren't quite what they expected for either one of them. Dale wasn't the golden boy anymore. He was just a married man who did tune-ups at Gilbert Chevrolet. He had to make payments on the trailer, pay the utilities, and Sharon got pregnant and was morning sick every day. But Sharon was happy with that. He was hers, and that was more than she'd ever dreamed. Then she got that phone call a day later while Dale was at work.

"May I speak with Dale please?" It was a woman's voice. She told me about it.

"No, Dale's at work. Can I take a message?"

"Well, I found his wallet. Would you have him give me a call?"

"Found his wallet?"

"It was behind the chair, and I didn't find it till I was cleaning up this morning. Is this Dale's mother?"

"I'm Dale's wife." She said that for a minute she thought it was funny, being mistaken for Dale's mother.

"Oh!" the other woman said and hung up. Sharon said the surprise in the voice told her all she needed to know. That's when she called me. I suggested it might've been Colleen Stephens, Marv's wife, but Sharon said she knew Colleen. So I went right over. I told her to call Dale at work and get it straightened out. She said she knew right away from his voice what was up. She said he'd better come right home.

Those things happen. Most of the guys I know drink a bit. They worked it out, and Sharon asked me not to tell anyone about it. She said Dale cried and said he was sorry. I can't imagine Dale Eggers crying, but Sharon said he did. She wanted me to believe it, and I said it was just between her and me. I said, "Sure. Those things happen." But Dale knew what he was doing.

Things seemed to go all right for a while, but Sharon didn't talk to me as much as she had before. She had a miscarriage, and I didn't even find out about it till a week after. I knew about Dale, and now she wanted to pretend it hadn't happened. But then, I'd started going with Ray Parker, and Ray is fun. Ray is probably the funniest man I know. He won a contest at the Cottage Bar in White Cloud as being the funniest man in Wabaningo County. They had a night there where anybody could get up on stage and tell stories, and then everybody voted, and they gave out a trophy. It got pretty raunchy. Ray was about the raunchiest of them all, but everybody had to admit he was funny, and he won hands down. I was so proud of him, but I was kind of glad Sharon didn't come. I really love Sharon, but she is a little on the good side. Maybe Dale got bored with that. Sharon's my best friend, but I do realize it might be a little boring to live with her.

Sharon never said any more about it, but I knew Dale was still playing around. I hear things at Antonelli's. People talk when they get a few drinks in them. The woman's name was Charlene Decker. She comes in sometimes with these girls from Hesperia. They're all kind of brassy, all blondes out of the same bottle. Really. They wear a lot of eyeshadow and purple fingernail polish. And they talk.

"I heard that Dale's still married," this other girl said, and Charlene said, "He had to," which is a lie, "and if you could see his wife, you'd believe it. What a mouse. Dale and me snuck over to his trailer one night and peeked in the window."

"You did not!"

"Honest," Charlene laughed. "Dale said she whines all the time. She was sitting there in curlers and these really dumb pink slippers with little mouse heads on 'em, not even watching TV, just sitting there staring at the wall with a book on her lap. He just can't hardly stand to go home anymore. He said that when they'd have sex it was like she was doing him a favor."

What could I do? I couldn't tell Sharon things like that. I could only be her friend. I called her up and went over the next day. I started going over a lot. She was alone almost every night. Dale's fooling around wasn't a secret anymore. Everyone talked about it. Everyone but Sharon. I think maybe it was pride. She didn't want to admit she'd been a fool, that it had been too good to be true after all. Dale Eggers just wasn't her type. She thought that was a reflection on her, but it wasn't. Charlene was Dale's type. Charlene was about what Dale would've been if he'd been a woman. He was good looking, but he couldn't make you laugh like Ray. Strange how what you want changes.

I got Sharon started in softball. She needed something to get her out of that trailer, and I could never get her to go to a bar. She wasn't the bar type, and I think she was afraid she might see Dale and Charlene.

She wasn't much good at softball, but then none of us were. Antonelli's was the joke of the Women's Independent League. But we had nice uniforms, and we had a lot of fun. We even beat Birch Hill Orchards one night when they only had eight players show up. Sharon made two nice catches in right field. In the bottom of the last inning, she came up to bat with two out and drove in the winning run. Everyone was cheering and slapping her on the back, and she was so happy she almost took it in stride when she looked up in the stands and saw Dale trying to sneak out of there with Charlene. "Do it!" I told her.

She smiled and gave me a great big hug. "We won," she said. "Let's go to the bar."

"Let's," I said and hugged her again. She was beaming and she had tears in her eyes, all at the same time. It made her look prettier than I ever thought she was.

ELINOR

I find myself thinking about Rome a lot lately. I've been listening to Respighi, and I'm on a balcony or terrazza with my morning coffee, looking out over the tiled roofs and basilicas as the city comes to life. So much of my life has been given to places like Cleveland or Pittsburgh or St. Louis, wherever Nelson had to be for sales meetings or conventions.

We did go to Rome together once. He gave in to my pleading and sulked through three days of it, but after finishing the European edition of the *Herald Tribune*, it was agony for him. He'd write down and total up the things he'd seen as if he were collecting points for a merit badge. "Okay, we've done that," he said after hurrying me through the Vatican Museum. We'd planned to spend a week in Rome, but he took to snapping his fingers and pacing up and down our hotel room, talking about all the things that had to be done at the office.

In the circles in which he moved, he was somebody. Chairman of the Board of Clark's, and Brainard's most prominent citizen. When he traveled, he had to have a purpose. His agenda was laid out for him, and the managers of the hotels he stayed in would welcome him personally. He had men who respected and feared him, who reaffirmed his importance. But

I don't believe Nelson had any real esteem in himself. A good earnings report told him who he was. *The Wall Street Journal* was an unfailing barometer of his confidence. You could look up the price of Clark's and tell what kind of day he was having. When the price was up, he was expansive. He would take me out to dinner in Muskegon or at the Club, and he was likely to notice things around the house, flowers I'd cut from the garden or a rearrangement of furniture. He would call me Ellie at times like that. He would lean in over the table and rub his hands together and say, "Ellie, we really should spend more time together, just the two of us." But when he said really, I knew it meant not really, and when the price fell or there was a drop in our brand share, the softness disappeared. His stride became longer, his posture more erect, and he paid no more attention to anything I said than he would to the singing of a bird.

And when he retired, it all seemed to turn around on him. I'm sure he was happy to see the company doing well, but when they'd report record earnings, it haunted him with the thought that they were getting along without him. That's business. They presented him with a plaque that said, whereas this and whereas that, that he'd been a giant in the industry, and all the men he'd dominated made speeches about what a great guy he was. But I suspect what they'd meant was, it was great to have him out of the way and a relief not to have to live in fear of him anymore.

When I met Nelson in Chicago, just after the war, he'd returned from the Navy to his engineering job with Food Equipment Company. He was intent on his work back then, but it wasn't the obsession it was to become. My brother Carl worked for F.E.C. and got me a job as a secretary with the engineering department. I'd begun my studies at the Art Institute. I had an idea I might someday be a painter, like Georgia O'Keeffe or Thomas Hart Benton, but we'd just come through a war and a depression, and my father persuaded me to a more practical secretarial course.

Nelson was twelve years older, and I was attracted by his re-solve. When he would pick me up for a date, he'd have decided exactly what we were going to do. "I've made reservations at the Pump Room for 7:30, and then we'll go over to the Chez Paree at 10:00 to catch the Jack Eigen Show. You'd like that, wouldn't you?"

Of course I liked whatever he suggested. What did I know? I'd grown up in Winnetka. I thought I'd like to be Mrs. Nelson Place. It seemed the most natural thing in the world. Nelson had a career. He was good-looking, considerate. My parents approved.

We rented a duplex in North Chicago, and I quit my job. I thought, with time, we'd get a house in Evanston. I thought I'd join the Junior League and that life would go on pretty much the way it had before the war, the life my parents had lived. I was twenty years old. Then, six months later, I discovered I was pregnant. I had morning sickness almost every day, and Nelson started traveling. He would take the train up to Michigan on a Monday and be gone two weeks. He was overseeing the instal-lation of new pureeing equipment for a thriving little apple products company called Clark's. I wouldn't say I was happy, but I had the baby to think about, and a month after Timothy was born, Nelson told me we were moving. He'd been hired away by Clark's as Chief Engineer. The money wasn't any more than he'd been making at F.E.C., but the chance for advancement was great, he said, and that's how we came to Brainard.

I thought that was the end of the world. Clark's sent a car down to meet our train in Grand Rapids on a drizzly, snowy evening in November. We drove for over an hour through forests and past dreary little farms, and when we got there, the first thing I noticed was the smell of cow manure. There was a tractor pulling a spreader ahead of us just south of town, and clods of manure got up under the fenders of our car and even on the windshield. It seemed emblematic of what my life had become. The driver cursed under his breath and I started to cry. I felt Nelson straighten himself and pull away from me. He pretended to be absorbed by whatever we were passing on the street. Then finally he turned back to me and said, "Elinor. Evanston, Illinois is not the world."

But that was almost forty years ago. I like Brainard now. It's still pretty provincial; people say "folks" when they mean "people," and I'd go mad if I couldn't travel, but I've got friends here, and memories. There's one thing Peter taught me, that if you travel as far as you can in any direction, this is the place you'll end up. So, in a sense, anywhere you are is the center of the universe. I think Peter came along at just that time in my life when I might've killed myself out of pure boredom. Old Mr. Clark had stepped down and named Nelson his successor, and the kids were off on their own. There was a time when I wouldn't have been able to bear the guilt of seeing another man. A hussy, that's what my mother would've called someone like me. But at that point I really didn't care. It was simply a matter of survival. Nelson and I had everything I thought we'd ever want, and it just didn't mean very much. I'd given up a lot to help Nelson get where he was, and I was drowning in the predictability of it: the sales meetings, the award dinners, the conventions, the ubiquitous odor of sterno, the smiling, the slow death.

Peter came to Grand Rapids to conduct a consciousness workshop at the River Street Church. "Being You," it was called. It came at a time when I thought that if I had to host another bridge party or two-ball foursome I would kill someone, just for a change of pace. I didn't expect anything to come of it, but with my first glimpse of Peter, everything changed. There was something about his eyes. There was no judgment in them, and, in his presence, I gave up judging myself. He ran his hands down my spine to correct my posture, and I shivered at his touch. I felt a kind of excitement I hadn't thought possible, and Peter felt it too. "Let your tension flow out into my hands," he whispered. "My hands are magnets."

After the first session of the workshop, I stayed to talk with him. It was as if I'd discovered some medicine I had to have in order to stay alive. I asked him out to dinner. Nelson was away on business, and I called and left word with our housekeeper that I'd had car trouble and wouldn't be home that night. I'd never done anything like that before. "Elinor," I told myself, "this is insane," but I didn't believe it. I think it was the first time I'd felt real desire.

And after that, I had the courage to begin traveling on my own. My pretext was always art, exhibitions in whichever city Peter was conducting a workshop, and Nelson indulged me.

He was traveling a great deal himself, and I think it eased his conscience. He'd had only one affair that I knew of, a young woman in Washington, with the FDA. One of her letters came to the house by mistake.

Peter was forty, and I was fifty-two. I still had my looks, I'd been careful about that, and of course, I had money. But whatever it was that attracted him didn't matter to me. He was my teacher, my soulmate. Nelson couldn't help making jokes when he'd see me in leotards, practicing my yoga in the living room. "I see you're at your karma quivers again," he'd say, or, "Just don't get natural on me, Elinor. I can't stand anything natural." Nelson had begun to seem old to me, and I really didn't think of Peter as a younger man. He was a strong man, but without ambition, unlike any of the men I'd known. He taught me to appreciate things just for what they were and opened my eyes to ways of seeing I'd lost as a child. "Don't look for answers, Elinor," he said to me. "Just learn to live with the questions." And I remember him picking a dandelion up out of the grass and handing it to me. "Just this, Elinor," he said. "Just this."

I wanted to be discreet; I didn't want to hurt Nelson's ego. I traveled to meet Peter in New York or San Francisco or Dallas or Palm Beach, and once we met in New Delhi and once in Hong Kong. My traveling got to be kind of a joke in Brainard, but not because anyone suspected I had a lover. I cultivated the image of an art maven. I do care about art, though. I care a great deal, and it's something Peter and I shared. He taught me to appreciate the subtleties of Oriental art, and I taught him about the Renaissance and the Impressionists.

Nelson didn't have time to come with me on any of my trips, and after he was forced to retire, he didn't have the patience. I always begged him to come along, but I knew he'd say no. He needed to be where he was known. "I just can't go gallivanting off like that," he'd say. They made him President of the Pine Lake Country Club and President of the Kiwanis, and as age forced him off one board after another, he actually seemed to get smaller, as if, bit by bit, the man was being taken away and only the empty costume remained. He began setting tasks for himself. He decided he would walk to every address in the Episcopal Church Directory. He found each one and checked it off. And when he'd completed that, he started in on the Brainard telephone book. He was just beginning the D's when he had his stroke. You store up that much frustration and something has to give. A vessel popped somewhere in his brain, and he doesn't know anything anymore. He smiles sometimes when I go to see him, the way a baby smiles when something bright is held over its crib, but I don't think he knows who I am. Maybe it's a blessing; I don't know. He doesn't seem to be suffering.

Sri Rananda says that until you have learned to find happiness in doing absolutely nothing, you will never be happy in anything you do; you will only be a spectator to this life. Nelson was afraid that if he wasn't doing something he would simply cease to exist. Now he stares at a grey tile floor all day long. Maybe he sees something nobody else can see, but I doubt it. I read in a book Peter gave me on Chinese characters, how there's no such thing as a symbol just for man. The man is always taking some action: man walking, man talking, man working. There's even a character for man enjoying the warmth of the sun.

Peter wanted to marry me, and I said no. I'm Mrs. Nelson Place; I always will be. Without the security marriage offered, his interest waned. It was inevitable. It may well have happened even if we had married. I won't kid myself about that. Eventually he met a younger woman, and she travels with him now, but I don't hold that against him. He was there when I needed him. We never could have come out into the open about it anyway. I've got the children to think of. Timothy's in San Diego. He's a commander in the Navy and might be an admiral someday. Ellen and her family are in Kansas City. I spend two weeks a year with each of them. I take the grandchildren to the zoo, I buy them presents. I do everything I can to spoil them.

I've been thinking of taking an apartment in Rome. To be there in the spring or in the fall when the tourists have gone, to spend afternoons drinking cassis and watching people on the Via Veneto, to get up early and walk through the Borghese Gardens, to watch the sun come up over the Palatine Hill and hear the birds begin singing. There's something about being out of the country. You feel you can do what you want to do, and you don't have to explain to anyone, even though it might not be anything you wouldn't do at home.

ROY

We don't know what really happened with Roy. I guess maybe we never will. I walk out in the fields sometimes in the evening, and I think of what it was like, how it wasn't just Thad, and it wasn't just Roy.

When the pounding started I was still lying in bed, but I wasn't sleeping. I'd forgotten the contractor was coming to start work shoring up the porch roof. He'd said he wanted to get started early, before the sun got too hot. It's an old house, Roy's family farm, and little by little we were fixing it up. I got up and asked the man to hold off for a while. I asked him in for some coffee. I told him I wanted to let Roy sleep, and I fixed him some bacon and eggs to take up the time.

Roy would make a run to Pennsylvania with a load of apple-sauce for Clark's, then swing back through Indiana to pick up a truckload of empty glass. He'd be gone about five days, then home two. Sometimes he'd drive to Texas for melons, sometimes to Iowa, sometimes to Kentucky. Until Thad came along, I thought Roy and I were happy. I thought that was the way life was.

Thad was interested in birds. It was one of the first things he noticed after I'd given him coffee, the *National Geographic Field Guide* on the counter by the toaster. He said he had one just like it and a lot of others too. He said the books had been one thing he'd made sure he got when it came to the settlement. Some of them were pretty valuable, he said.

You wouldn't have figured Thad for a birder, but then you probably wouldn't have thought I was either. Thad's a roofer mostly, though he does about any kind of carpentry. He just specializes in roofs. I talked to him about the barn roof too while he had his breakfast. Roy and I didn't farm ourselves; we did it on shares with Norris Wheeler, and we needed the barn to store our part of the hay.

It started out with birds and then got into all kinds of things. I told him how I'd gone out in one of the hay fields after it had been cut and raked into windrows. I'd gone out to look for bob-olinks, and when I'd stopped to watch a male preening along the fence line, I heard something, a kind of little ticking sound, and how I bent down and listened real close, and it was the hay drying. I told him how Roy thought that was funny, that he thought I spent too much time alone and maybe ought to get a job or do some volunteer work, but Thad didn't think it was funny.

"I believe that," he said. "I believe you can hear just about anything if you listen close enough."

I hadn't intended to get into that kind of conversation with a man who'd just come to fix the porch, but that's how it started. He was telling me about his son who'd broke the state record in the shot put when I heard Roy stirring and figured I'd better take him up his coffee. Kevin Decker. I'd read about him in the paper. I wouldn't have figured Thad would have a son that old. When I came back down, he told me how hard it'd been since the divorce, just seeing the kids on weekends, how his wife had married an insurance man who bought them almost anything they wanted and took the younger ones to Deer Park Funland twice a month and how he couldn't compete with that on what he made roofing.

ROY LIKED THAD RIGHT AWAY. He asked him to stay for lunch, and spent most of the afternoon helping him tear out the old rafters which had warped and were sagging pretty bad. They got the whole roof off and started fitting new support posts before quitting time. Roy and I were going over to the Valley for pizza, like we did most Saturdays there wasn't a Vegas Night at the Moose. I asked him if it'd be all right if Thad came along, and he said sure.

Roy and I didn't talk much when we were alone. There just wasn't much to talk about. He'd come home from a trip and tell me something funny that happened on the road or at some truck stop, we'd make love, and then that'd be about it till the next time. I'd tell him about seeing an owl or a fox or about something that happened on the farm, and he'd say, "Oh." Maybe his being on the road is what kept us together so long. I could never tell what he was thinking.

But with Thad around, Roy talked a lot. He talked about baseball and the economy and things I hardly knew he thought about. They talked about growing up on farms and peeing on electric fences, and as the evening got on into the third pitcher of beer, they even talked about birds. Roy didn't know much, but he seemed interested when Thad talked. Thad talked about eagles, about having found a nest in a big white pine tree near Walloon Lake and finding rabbit skulls and deer legs and pike skeletons maybe three feet long on the ground beneath it. I think it was about the best night I remember since we got married. I think Roy thought so too. With Thad there we laughed instead of just getting quietly drunk and going home to fall asleep in front of the late late show.

I remember a man came in wearing a cowboy hat, and he stood at the bar near our table. He stood facing us with his elbows back on the bar, and he had a belt buckle that said, "DICK," in big brass letters. "Big Dick," Thad said. He and Roy brought that up three or four times as the night went on, and we laughed about it. Then when we were leaving the bar, Roy decided he had to take a leak. Thad suggested he wait until we got out in the country, but Roy unzipped his fly and did it right there in the parking lot. Thad and I got the giggles. I think he might've been a little bit embarrassed, the two of us just standing there while Roy hosed down the blacktop. We put our arms around each other, just playing, but I could feel the tension. I gave him a little kiss on the neck before we let go, and just then was when the spotlight hit us. Roy finished and got zipped up just about the time Sergeant Kemp from the Sheriff's Department got there with his flashlight. He shined it around on the ground, and then shined it on Roy's face and issued him a warrant to appear in court on a charge of disorderly conduct. That's what cemented it with Roy and Thad. There might've been a fine involved, but mostly it would've been embarrassing to have that in the District Court Report in the paper. Two weeks later in front of Judge Bruckner, Thad testified that Deputy Kemp had neither smelled nor tasted the fluid in question to determine that it was urine and that what in fact had happened was that we'd found a half-full bottle of beer on the hood of our car and that we were just pouring that out on the pavement when the deputy came along. The judge threw out the case, and Roy thought Thad was a genius.

IT GOT TO BE A REGULAR THING, having Thad around. When the porch was finished, we had him start in reroofing the barn. I'd have him stay for lunch and sometimes dinner, sometimes when Roy was gone on a run, and I didn't want to make a secret about it. Roy called one Sunday night from Cleveland to tell me he'd had a breakdown and would be a day late getting home. I told him Thad was here for a late dinner, that we'd been out looking for a pileated woodpecker he'd spotted near Hesperia, and Roy said fine. He said he wouldn't get home until Tuesday and that the All-Star Game would be on TV Tuesday night and to invite Thad over to watch it with him. We got to be a threesome that way.

Sometimes Thad would be here late, but I never let him stay the night. I didn't want his pick-up here in the morning. People would talk anyway. It got back to me through Phyllis Wildfong. She just had to tell me, she said. People were saying, is Roy blind or what? I didn't care what they wanted to say. I've heard enough about myself to know that people will make up stories when they don't have any. So what's the difference? All I knew was that I was feeling things I hadn't felt in years. I cared about being pretty because of Thad, and when Roy was home, he appreciated that too. It made things better between Roy and me, made it new again. Roy would come home, and the three of us would spend time together. Sometimes it'd get late and Thad would sleep over. It might have been a little hard for him when I'd go off to bed with Roy. The walls in the house aren't that thick, but it was Roy's house. Thad knew that in a couple of days Roy would be on the road again. And Roy never talked about it. I figured he knew or else he didn't want to know. You could never tell what Roy might be thinking. He never got real happy or real sad, but he liked Thad. He liked me. We all liked each other.

THEN LAST OCTOBER THEY FOUND Roy's rig along U.S. 12 where it crosses the Prairie River near Burr Oak. It wasn't on his regular route, wasn't an expressway, but he'd take secondary roads sometimes to break up the monotony. There was a flat tire on the cab, and they found his clothes, his wallet, his sunglasses and his cap on the passenger seat. It'd been unseasonably hot, up near 90, and they figured maybe he'd gone down to the river to cool off before getting help with the tire. They wondered if it might've been suicide, if he might've been depressed, but you don't plan a flat tire. Maybe he didn't know how strong the current was. Thad drove me down there to the spot where the truck was, and the stream looked calm enough to me, but the sheriff said it could be deceptive. They never did find his body. Those rivers are deep and the bottoms are laced with fallen trees. It could be snagged down there somewhere. Maybe it isn't there at all.

THAD AND I DECIDED we wouldn't see each other for a while. I didn't know if I should be in mourning or what. People came by to offer their condolences; Roy's brothers, Dewey and Fred, Phyllis, other drivers for the company and their wives. My folks came up from Lansing and we brought Mr. Brande, Roy's dad, from the county home. Everyone brought food, and we had a kind of a wake. I didn't want any kind of service. I still don't know for certain that he's dead, and it might take years for the insurance company to settle.

Thad and I talked about it. It was all we talked about. We tried to get back together, but somehow it didn't feel right without Roy. We felt like someone was listening in on everything we said. Finally we gave it up, and a few weeks later Phyllis said she saw Thad at the Moose Thanksgiving Party with Kari McCormick.

This spring Thad moved to Mount Pleasant. He went in with his brother who's a builder over there, and I got a job at Clark's in the steno pool. I need the income now that Roy's gone, and Roy always said I needed something to do.

THINGS ARE CLOSER
THAN THEY APPEAR

The house is so clear to me now; it doesn't matter whether it was really there. For me it's as real as the eggs I had for breakfast. And the woman I met there, as real a presence as my mother who died and still talks to me whenever I think about her. "Shit flows both ways," she might say, if I am thinking about saying something bad about one friend to another or venting my anger at the total venality of my sister Alice's husband, Gordon, who sees everything, human or otherwise, in terms of dollar signs. There I go again.

My mother might remember the house, on the corner of Compton and Main, only a block from where we lived. It was a vacant lot all my life, grass and a few big maples. It looked like a park without benches, and we used to play ball there. I'd ask my mother about it, but like I told you, she died, and so my memories of the house must be hers as well. Funny how the mind works, how it goes on in others. I can hear her say, "It's all meat and no potatoes." She said that when I discovered psychology and told her how I had this anima, they call it, or ideal woman inside me and had to live out what she wanted if I wanted to be whole. Stuff like that. "All meat and no potatoes." She would say that about Nadine—that's an unusual name, isn't it?—the woman I met in the house. The funny thing is I've never known anyone named Nadine, so where did I get that if it wasn't really Nadine?

She was just sitting there in her nightie, brushing her long black hair. I didn't see her at first and wouldn't have walked up onto the porch if I had. I thought the house was deserted. I wouldn't just walk up to someone's house without a good excuse. I care what people think, and I wouldn't want somebody to say, "Whadda you want?" if they found me on their porch and not have any good reason to say back. They could call the police.

But since this house was deserted, or I thought it was, it was okay to explore. It was a big white house with a turret on one corner that went up three stories to a pointed roof. That part of it looked like a castle. And there was a long porch on two sides, one on Main and one on Compton. Everyone knew it was deserted, so I didn't think anything about going inside. I wanted to see what it looked like to look out the upstairs windows. That's mostly what I think of a house; how does it look from the windows?

It was that kind of an overcast day in late summer when the air is heavy and still and the green of the trees is darker and greener than it ever really is. I walked up the porch and stopped to look out at the street from there when I heard Nadine say, "It looks like rain, don't it?" That's the way she said it, incorrect like that, and I wasn't sure if she meant it that way or was just being funny. And then I heard the brush running through her long black hair and realized I'd been hearing that sound even before she spoke, though I hadn't paid any attention to it. It was that kind of whisper sound, quish, quish, through her hair, as regular as raking leaves. She leaned her head to the side and pulled the hair out away from her with the brush. She sat there in a white wicker chair, wearing a long white nightie, brushing her hair and looking out at the street as if it was natural for me to be there, as if I'd walked out of the house onto the porch instead of just up from the sidewalk.

"Yes, it feels like rain," I said, and it felt all right to be there. I didn't feel like I had to explain.

"Humm." She said it like a long sigh. "I love it like this, just before it rains. The air's thick as butter."

The air thick as butter. Imagine that. It felt so peaceful to be there on the porch, waiting for the rain. A horse clopped up the street, pulling a wagon that said "Scott's Dry Goods" on it, and even that didn't bother me. Just curious, I thought.

And then she looked at me, and I don't think I've ever seen eyes that green. "You look funny," she said.

"Funny?"

"Kind of lost," she said, and then she smiled, and I felt grander than I ever have before, and I wondered if I was the same person, to be smiled at that way. "Like you came out here to say something important, and now you can't think what it is." She gave a little laugh as she said it, and I felt like a movie star, she thought so much of me. I could tell by her smile. "Ha!" I laughed. "I guess I did." I felt so happy, and it was going to rain. I felt like my shoes belonged on the grey boards of the porch, and if there had been something I was going to say, I didn't care.

"Are you ready to go upstairs?" she asked. Her eyes were so

green. "I love it upstairs when it rains." I watched her hair float past me, so shiny from brushing, and I watched it float down her back as we climbed the stairs. The wood was dark and the walls, but her hair shone black, a bright black against the white of her gown, and she smelled like mint or sassafras. The steps creaked under our feet, and I heard the first rumble of thunder just as we turned the landing. Mother must love this house, I thought. Isn't it strange, not "would love" but "must love." I know she does.

The hall was dark, too, but then the sky was dark outside, and the door frame of the bedroom was massive, a big heavy dark molding, like in old banks or museums.

She folded back the covers of the bed. It was a brass bed, a big one with lots of white pillows and the white sheets folded back over the cotton quilt. There were blue flowers on the quilt. "You get into bed," she said. "I'll be back in a minute."

I always feel funny getting undressed. Men look so comical without clothes on. I've thought that in locker rooms, all so different and yet so much the same, cocks hanging there like vestigial tails. "Cover that thing up," Mother would say when I was little. "It's a shock for a girl to see a thing like that. You keep covered. We ain't savages."

It was warm in the room, and the sheets felt cool as I crawled in. I covered myself with the quilt and thought of how Nadine's feet sounded on the bare wood floor as she tiptoed out of the room and how I'd heard a little crack from her ankle. It felt so cozy in that big bed with the sky dark in the afternoon and the leaves swaying heavy in the maple outside the window. There was a pitcher and a basin on the dresser and a long oval mirror. There was a straightback chair in the corner and not much else in the room.

When Nadine came back, she went right to the window and opened it, and the room was full of the sound of the wind swishing through maple leaves. The white curtain billowed away from the window, and when she turned and smiled at me I felt like a king propped up on all those pillows. "You look so angelic," she said. "If I didn't know you. . . . You look so innocent." And I felt innocent, and I felt secure and at home.

She pulled her nightie up over her head. Her back was to me, and her hair almost covered her hips, but not quite. She turned around, and her breasts swayed forward as she put one knee on the bed. Her belly curved out over the black hair of her sex, and there was a little appendectomy scar on her abdomen. She slipped in beside me, and I wanted more than anything to kiss that scar. The scar made her so dear to me at that moment, remembering how she'd suffered and how brave she had been, how the snow whipped through the branches of the tree and how long it seemed to take for the doctor to come, how I'd held the lamp for him, her little cries and the whiff of ether in the room. And her little cries now as I kiss her there, the little rib of pink flesh, and then the dark springy mound of hair below it, and breathe in the deep sweet smell of her sex. I slide up, and she pulls my head to her breasts. I feel her tremble, and she holds me there, kissing my hair as the thunder breaks again and the lightning and the hissing of the leaves in the wind.

SMALL TALK

It's surprising how difficult it is for people to talk about the most important things. Since Emily's been gone I've felt restless most of the time, like nothing's really happening to me. We had insurance on each other's lives, one of those business protection policies we took out when we started the agency. I got $200,000 in the settlement, and the phone started ringing off the wall. People I didn't even know were hitting me up with hard luck stories and everyone had some idea how I could invest it. There were women who came on to me, women who probably wouldn't have paid any attention before. Some of them were beautiful, but they were women you knew would roll right over you if you got in their way.

WITH EMILY IT WAS ME and the children. She made us her career. She was in the business with me, on paper, but for her it was just showing houses once in a while. Now it seems like I'm lonely all the time, even when I'm with another woman. Even if we're making love, it's not like it was with Emily, not like we're friends who enjoy pleasing each other. Of course it took years for us to get to where it was like that, years of hurting each other and coming close to calling it off. We grew up together.

We got married young and grew up with the children. And at times when it seemed there was nothing holding us together, there were memories.

The last time I saw her she was heading out of town on her way to Grand Rapids to get her hair done. I was just coming in from showing a house down on the Muskegon, and as our cars passed I waved and she waved back. Just a hand through the glare of the windshield. She'd told me she might be late, and I'd said I'd take care of dinner. I had a couple of frozen burritos on a cookie sheet, ready to go into the oven, but it got to be eight o'clock. She hadn't gotten home, and I was beginning to get angry because she hadn't bothered to call. I put the burritos in the oven, figuring she'd certainly be home by the time they were done, but she wasn't. I ate my burrito and kept hers in the oven at 150. I dug out a couple of scoops of vanilla ice cream and sat down to watch a movie on TV when the dogs started barking. I got up and saw it was a State Police car, and I knew right away why they'd come.

The next morning I found that bowl of melted ice cream on the kitchen counter and the burned-up burrito in the oven, and when I think of that night, those are the images that come to my mind, that and her hand behind the windshield, waving.

For a couple of years after she died, I used to visit married friends, just to remind myself for a little while what it could be like. But later I felt sad because I couldn't imagine it ever being that way again for me. I didn't like going to bars. I tried that. I felt silly dancing, and I felt silly trying to make conversation, asking things like what movies they'd seen or what music they liked. I'd start listening to myself. I never did ask anyone what their sign was, and it wouldn't have meant anything if they'd told me. It was like we were all lonely people thinking maybe this is the one.

I WAS SHOWING A HOUSE when I met Joy. It was a saltbox colonial in one of the oldest subdivisions in Brainard, built back in the late forties. It was a nice house in what is now a nice neighborhood, too old to seem like a subdivision anymore. The houses on either side of it had been built off the same plans, although years of remodeling had given them each a more individual character.

Joy had taken her first teaching job at Maple Street School and was planning to move here from Detroit as soon as she found a place. It was early July, so she still had plenty of time to look around, but as I drove her back to the office, she told me she thought the house was just what she was looking for. There was something girlish about her and, at the same time, something sad. The sadness was in her eyes and in the little lines around them. Her face was round and fresh and flushed when she smiled, and her long brown hair, parted in the middle, made her seem younger.

"Where did you go to school?" I asked as we turned onto Main, and I thought, oh God, here we go again.

"Michigan," she said, "but that was twelve years ago. I got married and I never used my degree, so I went back to Wayne State last year and got re-certified."

I'd graduated from Michigan myself, and we made conversation about Ann Arbor and about drinking beer and making out in the Arboretum. I felt a little cheap talking about that because I remembered that it was in the Arboretum that Emily and I had first made love. I said something about U of M alumni being outnumbered in Brainard by Michigan State graduates. "We're in the land of the Udder University," I said and then couldn't believe I'd really said that, but she laughed, and it was okay. She gave me a hundred dollars earnest money to hold the house for a week while she went to the local banks to see if she could arrange financing, and I asked her if she'd care to have dinner with me. It wasn't business, I assured her, and I said something stupid about seeking solace among the barbarians. I hadn't given a damn about college loyalties in years, but she was gracious enough to agree that it sounded like a good idea. "Safety in numbers," she said. She told me she was staying at the Kincaid Motel just west of town, and I said I'd pick her up at seven.

After she left the office I began to wonder just where I intended taking her to eat. Brainard isn't exactly a culinary hotbed, and I didn't want her to think that, just because I was born here, I was a hick. I've been to New York. I've been to Mexico. I didn't want to treat her to the Salisbury Steak Special at Fred's or to take her to Antonelli's and have to introduce her to all the people there. It wasn't that they weren't people I cared about. It's just that they care about me a little too much. They want to see me happy. They want to see me married again, and they would begin sizing up Joy or any woman I was with the moment they saw her. I'd take her to Muskegon, I decided. Maybe she liked Chinese food. I thought it might make her feel a little more at home to be in a city, even a small city.

THAT HAD BEEN THE PROBLEM with Karen. Karen was from New Jersey and had lived in New York City ever since college. She had been Emily's roommate, and when Emily died, Karen came out for the funeral. Maybe it had been our memories of Emily that attracted us to each other. Karen and Emily had been very close, and Emily had gone to visit Karen in New York once a year in all but one of the twenty-two years we'd been married. I think Karen and I were searching in each other for traces of Emily, at least that's how it began. Karen came to visit four times in the year following Emily's death. We had been friends, but it seemed more and more, as we became lovers, that the friendship faded.

I'd always been curious about Karen. Everything about her seemed angular and a little hard-edged, her jaw, her hips, the quick decisive way she moved. Everything she did was deliberate. She was quiet, almost to the point of being sullen, and just the slightest bit cross-eyed. She and Emily were a strange pair to have been such good friends, but they found something in each other that brought them so close that, if I'd thought about such things at the time, I might have suspected they were lovers.

Karen and I didn't discuss marriage until her third visit, and when we finally did, it almost seemed as if it was something Emily would have wanted, as if somehow we owed it to her. I don't know if feelings can ever really be separated from memories, but I believed I was in love with Karen. There were things about her I didn't like, her sarcasm about Brainard and the kind of clipped way she had with my friends. "That's nice," she would say when they talked about their work or their families and then immediately change the subject and talk about *the* new restaurant in New York or *the* new disco. But when she would go back to New York, I couldn't stop thinking about her. I'd be working on an appraisal, and I'd find myself recalling the way she smelled or the look of her eyes when we talked about Emily, or the sounds she made when we were making love. In a way, I hoped I'd grow tired of her. I hoped that if we made love enough, I would get bored with it, and sometimes I would, for a day or two. But when she went back to New York, I missed her terribly, and I felt jealous of any other man she might be seeing there, though she claimed there was no one in particular.

Then after we'd discussed getting married, and she came out here the fourth time, everything that had seemed quaint or charming about rural Michigan on her earlier visits began to seem threatening. "It's so dark," she complained the second morning, after telling me she hadn't gotten any sleep at all. I've known city people who haven't been able to stand the quiet here. They'll pretend it's boredom, people who've spent their lives in cities with all the distractions, who feel threatened by the emptiness. It's the open fields and dark woods. The same things they might look for in a vacation spot will spook them if they think of it as a place to live.

We had dinner with Bob and Susan Murdock and spent the evening on Bob's float-boat on Brainard Lake, and driving back to my house, Karen said, "What do people do here, I mean to stay alive, to keep from turning into tree stumps? Your friend Bob talked about the slump in tractor sales till I thought I was going to scream. I could talk about public relations, but they wouldn't know any of the people I represent. I mean, my God, they don't know anything. Susan thought Elaine's was a dress shop. She said she thought she'd gotten a catalogue from them." I should have talked about it then, but I didn't want to spoil our time together. I didn't want to be alone again. And a week after she went back to New York, I got her letter telling me that we must've been kidding ourselves, that she could never live in my world and that she knew I couldn't live in hers. She was right, of course, and that was the end of it. I didn't even bother writing her back, and I think I was lonelier then than I had been that second week after Emily's funeral when everyone had gone back to their lives.

I KNEW IT WASN'T going to work out with Joy. I knew it wouldn't work because I wanted it to work. If I hadn't really cared, it might've been all right. I suppose someday I'll find some woman I don't care about, and then things will be okay. But if I don't care about her . . . Well, that's the problem. I'm just no good at small talk. I started right in with Joy, telling her about Emily, about how much I missed her, about the drunk who'd swerved over the center line, about the burritos and the melted ice cream, and Joy didn't say anything, or maybe she just said, "Oh."

When I asked her about herself, she seemed to loosen up. She told me how she met David, her ex-husband, when he'd come to pick up her roommate. Her roommate hadn't been ready and had asked Joy to go up to the dorm lobby to tell him she'd just be a few minutes. It had meant the end of their friendship, she said, but having David had seemed so important to her then that she had been willing to accept that as a consequence. She moved to another dorm, and a year later they'd gotten married and she'd given up her plans to teach. Her husband had gone into advertising and had made a good start with an agency in Detroit.

He'd explained it to her quite simply, she said. He and Louise—that had been the woman's name—were in love, he said, and they shared the same vocational interests. That's how he put it. After nine years, "We share the same vocational interests." She said she had thought about her former roommate then and wished, more than anything, they'd still been friends.

"Did you feel guilty?" I asked her. "I mean did you feel as though it was some kind of retribution?"

She looked at me as if she hadn't understood the question.

"I mean it sounds like you're better off without him, like he was just using you to get something he wanted more." I could see right away that I'd said the wrong thing. Her eyes got darker and her face lost its form, as if her cheeks had gone numb. I knew I shouldn't have started talking about Emily. I wanted to open my mouth and suck the words back in like bubblegum. I'd thought it would help her to talk about things; I thought it would bring us together, but she looked at me as if I was the one who had rejected her, and she started to cry. She hadn't even touched her mu shu pork. She said she was sorry and asked me to take her back to her motel.

"No, I'm sorry," I said. "I didn't mean to make you dredge all this up." And she didn't say anything after that. I turned on the radio in the car, but the music didn't seem right, so I turned it off. There was a full moon coming up, all orange above the horizon as we headed east, back toward Brainard. "Nice moon," I said, and then I wished I hadn't said it. I glanced over at Joy, and her head was turned, and she was looking out the window.

When we got back to the motel, I got out and opened the door for her. I thought I had a pretty good idea how she was feeling. I tried to give her a hug, just to be friendly, to let her know that I understood what she was going through, but I felt her stiffen up. "Good night, Joy," I said, and it was like saying good night to someone I'd just passed on the street.

I NEVER DID HEAR BACK from Joy about the house. She bought a small ranch style from another realtor. It's just two blocks from the one I showed her. I guess she's getting along all right. I saw her the Friday before Halloween as I was driving by the school. She was kneeling down on the playground, talking to a small witch who was crying. I've thought a lot about calling her up, but I don't think she wants to hear from me. She probably thinks I'm upset about the house deal, but I'm not. I would have even given her back the earnest money if she'd asked for it.

WHEN I THINK BACK ON ALL the years Emily and I spent together, I realize how much there was we never talked about. "A penny for your thoughts," she'd say. She must have said that a thousand times, and I'd almost always just shake my head or say, "Oh, nothing." We talked about what the children were doing in school or who they were dating. We talked about taxes, about houses we were close to selling and about the people who were buying and selling them. It's amazing how much you get to know about people by what they want in a place to live.

SHELTER

Because he'd been in Jackson Prison, he carried a kind of an aura about him. Men he'd known all his life would look at him and think, "He's been in Jackson," with all the mystery that name would conjure up for them, as if he were some character from a movie they'd seen, walking the streets of their town.

It was late October when Ray came back, a cold late October day with only a few leaves still clinging to the black trees and the ground camouflaged under leaves pressed flat with the rain. I remember thinking that the weather must have suited his mood as we neared Brainard, driving north, and the land began to break up into hills and woodlots. I knew his thoughts were on Karen and what might have happened to her. He'd had no word from her in over a year and must have felt abandoned by the whole world he had known before he was sent away. I had gone down to pick him up because no one else had offered to. He didn't say much on the way back, and I didn't know how I would initiate a conversation, didn't know what might interest or offend him, so we rode in an uncomfortable silence until we crossed the Muskegon River at Butler, and he said, "I don't know why, Ruth, but the river seems wider to me, wider than I remember it."

"It is wider," I said, and I laughed a little in relief. "They finished the dam down at Whiskey Creek."

I don't wonder that any time at all in a place like Jackson would have its effect on a person, so I wasn't surprised that he seemed harder, more distant, as if not quite sure this soaked autumn landscape wasn't just another of the illusions he must have lived by those three long years. I tried to imagine what it had been like for him. Twenty years before, I had taken Ray on as my special charge, and I knew he was no killer. He didn't do anything half the men in town wouldn't have done. The man in the bar had been going after Ray's brother with a pool cue, and Buck had probably deserved it. Buck was a bully all his life, the kind who took pleasure in causing pain and who didn't mind getting hurt in the process. The Halloween I had Ray in school, Buck was caught hanging Mrs. Melvey's calico cat by the neck from the cable over Main Street where they normally display banners for Heritage Days, the County Fair and the Santa Claus Parade. When he was caught, while the cat was still clawing the air above the street to the horror of a few late revelers leaving Bob's Bar and the policeman who apprehended him, Buck's defense had been, "It was only a cat."

Buck had been fooling around with the man's wife and had been bragging about it, Ray told me. He'd taunted the husband, challenging him to a fight if he didn't like it. I'm sure we'd all have been better off if Ray had just let the man bring the cue down on Buck's head while he was bent over the pool table, but Ray couldn't let that happen. He had thought of it as a noble gesture when he smashed the man with his beer mug. Of course he hadn't intended to kill the man; he was only protecting his brother, but he hit him twice, so they called it manslaughter and gave him five years.

I thought about Ray a lot while he was away, and several times I had a dream that I was in a grey stone cell from which there was no escape and then that I was waking up to find myself in the same bleak circumstances I had been dreaming. One night when he'd been drinking and I got him to talk about it, he told me that's how it had been, that he would lie there and think about Karen, worrying that something might happen to her, that she might be raped or killed in a car crash or get cancer and die before he got out. "There's no controlling what your mind will do when you're locked away like that and can't talk to anybody you care about," he said. He was sitting on the couch in my front room as he talked. His face had gone grey, and he pulled at his hands, as if to keep them from shrinking back in his sleeves.

RAY HAD BEEN IN HIS SENIOR YEAR when I started teaching at Brainard High. I'd taught four years over in East Tawas before coming here, and I was just nine years older than my oldest students. But Ray wasn't like any other student I'd had. He was a big raw-boned kid, but there was something fine about him, a kind of sensitivity you could discern only in his eyes. They looked out, with no bitterness, at a world that hadn't offered him much time to grow up. His mother, Sadie Christman, had quite a reputation around town, and his father had been in jail half a dozen times for beating her in public or for beating some man he thought she'd been fooling around with. Ray would come to my apartment sometimes, and I felt flattered when he did. He just wanted to talk. He couldn't talk to girls his own age, he told me. He said they laughed at him because he was so clumsy and would think he was weird if he tried to talk to them in the way he talked to me, and I believe they would have. He asked a lot of questions about women, questions I didn't quite know how to answer, like what did women think about sex and what was it they found attractive about men.

I used to worry what people might think about his being alone with me in my apartment so much, but I didn't want to discourage him from coming. I'm sure his sister Betty, who was four years older than Ray, suspected there was something going on. She came to see me at school one day after classes were over. "I hope you know what you're doing, Miss Dillard," she said, "because Ray doesn't."

"I don't know what you mean, Betty," I said. She had a purse in her hands, a kind of shoulder bag, and she twisted the strap around her hand as she talked so that it made white lines where it cut into the flesh.

"Ray idolizes you," she said. "I just wanted to be sure you understood that. He'd do anything you even suggested."

"I appreciate you telling me that, Betty," I said. "I only have Ray's interests in mind. Sometimes he just needs someone older to talk to."

She looked down at the floor. "Well, that's all I wanted to say, Miss Dillard," she said. She unwound the purse strap from her hand, turned and walked out of the room. All Ray and I ever did was talk, but my thoughts about him weren't all that innocent. There were times when I fantasized that when he came to see me he'd throw himself into my arms, and I would comfort him. That's how it would begin, but it never happened. I've fantasized about other students over the years but never so intensely as I did about Ray. I would hold my pillow in my arms after he had gone and remember his questions and the way his voice had broken when he asked them, and I would explore myself with my hands and I would think, "This is how a woman feels, Ray. This is for you."

I KNOW THERE'S BEEN TALK that I'm a lesbian. I guess there is about any woman who doesn't marry. For ten years I shared a house with Virginia Rives, and when she moved down to Tennessee everyone treated me like I'd been abandoned, but we were just two friends who shared expenses and lived quite separate lives. It used to be that a single woman was just an old maid, but now, if you aren't married or openly promiscuous, it's assumed that you're gay. I kind of lost touch with Ray a year or two after he graduated. Karen was a divorcée from Oceana County, and I only met her at the wedding. Ray got a job driving a forklift in the warehouse at Clark's, and I'd get a card from him on my birthday, and once in a while I'd see him on Main Street, and he'd give me a hug and tell me how happy he was with Karen and how everything seemed to be going all right for him. But when he came back from Jackson, his job had been filled, and they weren't hiring. People acted friendly to him, but it was a kind of friendliness born out of fear. They wanted to stay on his good side, but nobody wanted to let him get close. He'd killed a man, and he'd been in Jackson, and who knew what he might do. In principle everyone thought he should be given a chance, but nobody wanted to risk getting involved. There'd been too many horror stories on the evening news. When he ran into someone he had known, they were always on their way somewhere, he told me. "Good to see you, Ray," they'd say, glancing at their watches. Nobody wanted to bring up prison. "Nobody will look me in the eye," he said.

But the worst of it was that Karen was gone, and so was Buck. Her letters started tapering off about a year into his term, and after two years she stopped writing altogether. He knew she'd gone off with Buck because in all the letters he received, mine included, nobody had written about either one of them. "Karen's gone, and Buck's gone." That's all I could say when he put the question to me directly, and that was all I knew for certain. But I did know she'd been seeing Buck. I couldn't understand it, but then I never can. When Ray asked me what it was that women found attractive about men, I couldn't account for women like Karen. Maybe it was Buck's meanness that fascinated her. Some women think that if they can make a man want them enough, they can turn him around, the way they might break a mean horse. Or maybe it was the excitement of something that frightened her.

I had arranged a two-room apartment above the Mini-Mart for Ray on a month-to-month lease. I tried to get it for a year, but Don Proctor balked at that, even though he had known Ray since Ray was a child. "Let's just see how it works out," he had said. But Ray began spending more time at my place than he did at his apartment. At first it was just that he remembered how it had been twenty years before when he'd needed a friend, but I was past my concern with propriety, and it wasn't long be-

fore he'd moved in with me. We were both desperate, for quite
different reasons. I'm sure my students will be stunned when
word gets around. I'm sure they can't imagine that I ever think
about men in a sexual way. I'm fifty-two years old, and I'm not
sure what they think anymore. To them I'm Miss Dillard, and
I have a reputation for being tough, but if they get through my
College English, they know how to write. I only wish Ray
could have had me when I was young, when my stomach was
flat and my breasts hadn't started to droop. I wish we could have
come together because we wanted each other and not just because we're all we have. And I hope that maybe in time he'll
come to love me *because* I am a little bit faded, and because he
has suffered so much himself and will see that beauty isn't just
that one thing we thought it was when everything lay ahead
of us.

LAST NIGHT, AFTER HE'D rolled over to his side of the bed
and pretended to be sleeping, I could hear the quiet sniffling
and feel the convulsions, like little electric shocks in the mattress. But I didn't say anything. I didn't want him to get started
talking about Karen. I didn't want to get him into a rage. I
wanted to think I had drained all that out of him. I didn't want
to spoil the dream, and the next day Betty called.

"I know he'll be in touch with you," she said. "It's real important, Miss Dillard. I've got to talk to him."

Ray was in the shower when she called, and I told her I'd find
him and give him the message. I knew from the breathlessness
of her voice that it had to do with Buck and Karen. I knew if I
told him he'd be gone and there'd be trouble. In the terms of his

parole, he wasn't permitted to leave the state. I looked at the TV set, and I could imagine the report on the evening news: *A Brainard man has turned himself over to police in Chicago ...* There would be film of him in handcuffs, being stuffed into a police car, and people in Brainard would shiver and feel smart about having stayed clear of him.

Ray walked into the kitchen just after I had hung up the phone. He was drying his hair with one of my big pink towels, and he asked me who called.

"It was the principal," I said. "He heard the senior class was planning something pretty suggestive for the Christmas Pageant, and he wanted me to talk to them about it."

"Things don't change much, do they?" Ray laughed and put his arms around me and held me to his chest. He was still warm from the shower, and he smelled of my lavendar soap.

"Why don't we go somewhere this weekend," I said. "Why don't we go to Detroit. I want to go out to dinner with you and not worry about what anyone will think."

He bent down and kissed my hair, and I felt the strength of his arms around me, and I didn't feel any guilt about having lied to him. I don't know what's going to happen. If I can just make him care about staying alive. I don't even care if it means my job. A person has to take chances. I just wish I could make time go by faster, put a month behind us, six months, a year.

SUSPICION

Some nights I wake up from a sound sleep and wonder if Lisa's been fooling around. She's clever enough so I'd never suspect it if she was. I never can see a cow without saying "cow," myself. And what finally makes me suspicious is that I can't even remotely imagine her doing it.

I had an affair once, a woman with the firm, a legal secretary in our Lansing office. There was a period, a couple of years ago, when I'd been in Lansing two or three days a week. We had a class action suit against the state, a water pollution case, and it was on my first trip there that I met Rona. Funny, you think of the names of women with whom you might have an affair. Margo had always seemed the most likely name for me, or Julie or Deborah, never a Ruth, a Helen or a Grace. The name Rona was strange. I'd never considered it either way, and Rona was older, ten years older than me. There was the attraction of experience. She had been divorced twice, had two children in college, one at Smith and one at Stanford. They were both bright kids and may have won scholarships. And she had some money, considerably more than she made from the firm. At least one of her former husbands must have been wealthy, and generous. "They were both fine men," is all she'd ever say about them, though she did tell me that I bore a striking resemblance to her first husband and that that was what had first caught her attention. She said I looked so much the way he had looked at the time they were married that she'd felt a chill when she first saw me. "I was curious," she said.

She had a large Victorian farmhouse on a lake about ten miles from town, and she took me there on our first evening together. It was on my third weekly trip on the pollution case, and I'd asked her out to dinner. I'd realized the attraction when we were first introduced, but I have a fear of being presumptuous, and in our four years of marriage I'd never seriously considered another woman. "Rona, this is Bill Shaw. He'll be with us on the Bryerly Landfill case." Jim Kaufman, her boss, introduced us. "Well, hello," she said, holding her hand out over her IBM Selectric, more as if it were being proffered for a kiss than for the shake that occurred. It had the effect of making me feel like a celebrity, and since I'd only been with the firm two years and had achieved no remarkable distinction, it took me by surprise. Once, on a street in New York, I was mistaken for a wide receiver with the Jets by a very persistent autograph hound, and for the rest of that day and for several days afterwards I had the feeling, entering restaurants, that people were discreetly pointing me out to their companions.

When I asked her out to dinner, I was only playing at the possibility of having an affair. Mostly I was just a little lonely. The dinner invitations to the homes of the lawyers with whom I was working on the Bryerly case had been expended, and it had come down to the prospect of dinner alone in the hotel restau-

rant and an evening of reading studies of groundwater con-
tamination or of pointless TV. One of those evenings had been
enough, and I was almost desperate for companionship. I'd
rather be a garbageman than a traveling salesman. So I asked
Rona if she'd care to have dinner. I did it as casually as I could
manage so that if she declined I wouldn't feel foolish, like a rejected lecher, but I had to work against a noticeably accelerated
pulse rate.

"I'd love to," she said, so enthusiastically that I felt a little
foolish at having been concerned. We had a bottle of Montra-
chet to begin with and, after consulting each other about the
garlic, ordered escargots for an appetizer. We had a Cabernet
Sauvignon with a rack of lamb, and she said she'd been a bit
surprised and just slightly hurt that I hadn't asked her earlier.
"I love this early defensive circling part of an affair," she said,
"when it's all so innocent." I felt my pulse pick up again when
she said that. It was when she said "affair" that I knew I was
being drawn into a situation that I could probably not gracefully prevent from becoming serious.

But the wine had worked its effect: I felt continental, appreciated. If she had been younger or my own age, I probably
wouldn't have been able to raise my glass, smile knowingly and
toast, "To innocence." I might've been paralyzed by that image
of myself as a lecher. But because she was older, I was able to
feel that I was the one being persuaded, and that made it all
right.

"Tell me about yourself," she said. She took my hand and
leaned in over the table when she said it. "Are there any ten-

der spots, anything you're sensitive about, anything I should know?" It was obvious from the way she said it, from the smile, from her eyes, that it was physical spots and sensitivities she was talking about.

"Well, I'm sure there are," I said, "but I just can't think of them at the moment." This is wonderful, I thought.

"I love to explore these kinds of things," she said. "It's kind of like discussing the preparation of a fine dinner. It's half the enjoyment."

"And you?" I asked. "Do you have any special spots?" I'm not sure I felt bold. I think I felt obligated to ask, and I felt a flush rise in my face, imagining the not-quite-perceptible steam, the pent-up heat that might be let off when she unsnapped her bra and stepped out of her panties. She would know precisely what she wanted, and I was right.

"Give me just a minute," she said when we'd gone back to her house and she'd fixed me a drink. "I want to put some satin sheets on the bed." She kissed me on the temple. "I want this to be just right."

I spent the night, and what surprised me most was that I didn't feel any of the guilt or awkwardness I'd imagined I would. It was just all very pleasant, and I no longer packed for my trips to Lansing with that mild constriction of homesickness I'd had before I began spending my nights at Rona's house. And after the first night, the thrill wore off a bit, too. It was just very pleasant there in her house by the lake, and I felt at home, as if Rona and I had been married for a few years. We listened to music and played Scrabble or watched movies on cable TV.

I still checked into the hotel and I would mess up the bed and use the bathroom after I left the office and before we would drive out to Rona's. And I don't think anyone in the office suspected. I think we were both too comfortable with our arrangement to call attention to it. It was as if I were returning home when I came back to Rona's and returning home when I went home. And Lisa never suspected anything. In fact, that was the part that bothered me. If Lisa didn't suspect, wasn't it possible that she might be seeing someone else and that I would have no suspicions? I wondered about that, and it gnawed at me a little, a mild pain in the solar plexus, as if I'd eaten something that had gotten stuck there.

After four months of this very pleasant double life, I was taken off the Bryerly case. Our Lansing lawyers were ready to take it to trial, and because of the experience I had gained on it, the firm sent me to Traverse City, about three hours north. I was to assist in a case against a developer who had put substandard septic systems in his waterfront development on the East Bay.

Rona sent letters to me in care of the Traverse City firm I was working with, and I wrote to her at her home. It was lonely in Traverse City, and my loneliness made me think about Rona more than I would have had I been home. And it also made me think about Lisa. Sometimes I'd call home in the evenings, and more often than not there'd be no answer. Lisa always had a perfectly plausible explanation, but it occurred to me that I had always had plausible explanations the few times she said she'd called my hotel in Lansing.

One week Rona took a few days' vacation to meet me in Traverse City, and in this new setting our affair seemed new again, at first. But the second night I could see there was something sad about it. Rona seemed sad. I thought it might just be the fact that we probably wouldn't see each other again for a long time. But after making love, very pleasantly if without great passion, she told me that she'd met another man, a state senator from the Upper Peninsula, and that he was leaving his wife in order to marry her. He was her own age, and she needed someone to grow old with, she said.

"It doesn't mean that I might not see you again sometime, somewhere on neutral ground." She was lying back against the pillows. She held a cigarette very gracefully above the night table, and in the light from the TV she looked quite beautiful. "But for a few months, anyway, I've got to devote myself to Stephen, to getting our relationship established." I remember thinking that it sounded as if she were discussing plans to redecorate my room.

It felt funny to hear his name. Stephen. Rona lying in bed with someone named Stephen, talking with Stephen as she was talking with me now. And then I thought of how, if Lisa were seeing someone, he'd have a name too, and a body, and that she might be in love with him and find the thought of giving him up deeply painful. Lisa, caring about someone else, thinking about him while we were making love, pretending to be cheerful and attentive while missing him. I might never know, and that uncertainty became unbearable.

I'm not the kind of man who would hire a detective to check up on his wife. I don't want to turn what might be just a suspicion into a sordid business of spying and deceit. Lisa still seems devoted to me. I told you she was clever, and I probably never will know for sure. Maybe if I were certain it was really over with Rona, if I knew we wouldn't be seeing each other anymore, maybe then I'd tell Lisa about it. Maybe it would make her appreciate me more. Maybe then she'd tell me.

THE NIGHT IS
GROWING LONGER

Now in mid-August, our yard is almost screened by the dark green leaves of the maple whose limbs reach out below the window of my study. This second-floor room was Mark's until he went off to college, but now I've taken it over and made it my own private place. I keep my books here and my tapes, the Navaho chief's blanket I bought in Flagstaff the summer I took Gloria and the boys to the Grand Canyon, a reproduction of the painting of Van Gogh's room at Arles, the photo of Tobin when he was eleven with his record walleye at Saddle Lake in Ontario. These are the things I most care about.

Sometimes I write letters to Tobin. I tell him what I've been doing since he's been gone, about the things that occur to me, if for nothing else than to confirm he's still in my thoughts. In the last letter I told him how some mornings after I get off work, I drive north of town to the acres his mother and I bought when I was making a lot of money and where we thought we might build someday and how I spend hours picking up sticks and twigs from under the pine trees in the forest there and how it always seems that each time I do there are more to pick up than there were before and how I do it again and again and feel good about it. It's a practice I would've thought absurd a few years ago, but it's something I think Tobin could've understood. I tell him about the books I've been reading and the dreams I've had, things I wish I could tell Gloria. I put the letter in an envelope, with no return address so it can't come back, and mail it off to Tobin in Paris or Rome or Arles, or any other place I think he might've wanted to go.

From my desk, I can see over the canopy of maple leaves, beyond the board fence, into the Eckerts' yard next door. They have a barbecue down there and a lot of patio furniture, an umbrella-table and chairs, a glider and a chaise lounge, all plastic and aluminum. This window's like a balcony seat to a stage set on which nothing much happens. Most of my time here I spend sleeping. I get off work at 7:00 a.m. I work for Pinkerton's, looking after the office down at Clark's. Gloria calls it a failure of will, a loss of nerve, but for me it's freedom from a world I don't want anymore. I made a lot of money with Clark's and invested it well. Now I just want my routine, and the night to be alone in. I make the rounds from 11:00 p.m. on and key into the clocks every couple of hours, but most of the time I have free to read or just to enjoy the quiet. It's clean and strange there, like being in a space station orbiting the moon. It fairly hums with the emptiness. Everything's put away, every desk cleaned off. The only sign that anyone's been there are the papers in the wastebaskets. Sometimes I'll browse through them before the janitors come around. I make it a point to avoid the janitors. I make it a game, pretending they're the night watchmen and that I'm an intruder.

I wait till they've finished cleaning Jay Campbell's office, the one that used to be mine when I was heading up sales, and then

I go in there and read. I have all the time in the world to read, and I get a little exercise making my rounds.

The only other people in the building are in the Data Processing Pool, logging the daily reports from the district offices. They're all glassed in, atmospherically controlled. It's like visiting an aquarium when I walk past there, or a tableau in some museum of technology. I see them, but they seldom see me. Once in a while somebody waves, but I don't care. I just make my rounds. I don't want conversation. In my mind I might be walking in Paris or on the coast of Sierra Leone, depending on the book I've been reading. Last night I was walking the streets of Camargo with Pancho Villa, planning the attack on Zacatecas.

Gloria thinks I've gone a little crazy, thinks I should see someone and get help. But help for what? I think about her a lot when I'm at work, think of her at home in bed, warm in sleep like fresh-baked bread. Sometimes I want to sneak off for an hour or two and come to her in her dream, not even waking her as we make love.

Sometimes I can't stand it. I have to go down to the men's room and close a stall door and take care of myself. It's always her I'm thinking about, but I'm someone different every time. I'd like to sneak home, but I'd lose my job, and I need the discipline. It wasn't an easy job to get. They told me I was overqualified, but they finally gave in. And I know that if I really did sneak home, it wouldn't be the way I've imagined it. She'd simply be annoyed. She has to get up and go to work in the morning. And when I do see her, she's been sleeping and I've been making my rounds, and there's nothing to talk about really. I've

156

tried to tell her about the stories I've been reading, but it comes out sounding trivial, like gossip about people she doesn't know.

Gloria's gone a lot on the weekends. She started studying estate planning after Tobin died, went to work for the Frome Agency, and she's been tops in sales the last two years. She speaks at conferences and conventions. Sometimes she goes to Chicago to visit her mother, she says. I wonder if she's seeing someone.

This morning, over coffee and raisin bran, I told her about a fantasy I had. I was a general in the Mexican Revolution, and she was an American woman who had come to Guadalajara to tutor the children of an aristocrat. I told her how lately I've been thinking of sneaking off from work, and how I would become real in her dream. I thought she might at least be intrigued by the idea, but at 7:30 in the morning it didn't sound the way I'd imagined it, even to me. It felt rehearsed, because it was. I had to work myself up to telling her about it, and I felt my face get hot. My lips stuck to my gums. I heard myself talking, and I stopped halfway through. Gloria rolled her eyes. She was already dressed for the office when I got home: heels, makeup, earrings, her shiny brown hair pulled back in a twist. "You really have to think about some other kind of job," she said. "It isn't healthy to think like that. You could get on the third shift at the plant maybe. The hours would be the same. You need something to occupy your time, at least. You don't live in this world anymore."

"Sure," I said. "Can you imagine some foreman telling me to hose down the floor? They all know who I am. I was the Vice-President of Marketing for God's sake!"

"I can't imagine you doing what you're doing now," she said. "Other people go on living. You think it's been easy for me?"

I felt I had it coming. It wasn't what I'd told her so much as the way it had come out. I could smell her perfume across the breakfast table. "Couldn't we . . ." I started to say. "Couldn't you be a little late for the office?"

"Jeffery," she sighed heavily, "we can't start that."

"But we never start that," I argued. I could feel myself sinking, feel Gloria rising above me, as if she were growing larger and couldn't see me anymore.

"Okay," she said, "okay, okay."

She finished off the coffee in her cup and then she got up from the table. She pulled the curtains over the windows around the breakfast alcove. "Okay, Jeffery," she said. She undid her patent leather belt and coiled it up on the table. She rolled her beige knit dress up around her waist and pulled her panties and her pantyhose down around her ankles.

"Couldn't we go into the bedroom?" I suggested.

"Jeffery, please. I've got my makeup and my hair. I've got clients waiting for me." She stepped out of her shoes, pulled her pantyhose down off her left foot. She leaned over, put her hands on the corners of the kitchen table, and she spread her feet apart. "Come on," she said, "I want it this way." Her voice was matter-of-fact, as if she were telling me how she wanted the furniture rearranged.

"But Gloria . . ."

"Jeffery, you're the one who wanted it."

I walked around behind her. She was dry, and it was hard getting started. She held herself still, braced against the table, and

I felt as if I were doing calisthenics. The American governess had finally given in to the Mexican general, gone almost mad with passion, as if she were trying to punish or consume him. She even frightened him a little, this self-styled general who had come down from the mountains of Oaxaca and made the Federales fear his name. She was foreseeing his death in her frenzy, and he was letting go of his life, as he knew he must each time he led his men against Huerta. He wasn't the kind of general who looked down from the mountains.

"Come on over, Tobin," I said. "You can make it." He was as tall as I am and easily as strong. I'd crossed at that same spot just twenty minutes earlier. I'd been working my way upstream a little. I'm not sure about the time, but there was a poplar with the big branch drooping down to the water. It looked a little different from where I was, but there was a sand bar down there, and the water wasn't much above my hips when I crossed it. I couldn't understand why he seemed hesitant. "It slants off just a little, but the bar's good and firm," I hollered over the purling of the water. Tobin held his rod up with one hand, and he used his rod case as a wading staff with the other. "I'm coming, Dad," he called. He moved out into the current. It sounded like he gave a little laugh, and he was gone. I'm certain he was crossing at the same spot. There was that twisted poplar branch drooping down to the water.

I LOOKED DOWN AT THE RIDGE of her spine through the back of her dress, at the graceful swirl of her hair. She held herself rigid, as if any motion on her part might spoil the day. The table skidded slightly on its legs. Cold coffee sloshed in my cup, and then the pitcher tipped and its milky whiteness spread around the saucers and bowls and seeped into my crumpled paper napkin.

"Oh shit," she sighed.

"Don't worry," I said. "I'll clean up."

"Are you about finished?" she asked. She turned her head toward her shoulder.

"I'm done," I said. I stopped my rocking against her. I stood still a moment, and then I slipped out of her.

"I didn't feel you come," she said.

"I didn't."

"Well I want you to," she insisted. She took her position again.

"It isn't going to happen," I said.

"You're just doing this to prove a point, Jeffery."

"Maybe I am," I said.

I WENT TO THE WINDOW and watched her getting into her Buick. I admired her long legs as she bent to put her attaché case on the seat before getting in. She fastened her seat belt and closed the door. Her hair was perfect, her face not the least bit flushed. I watched her stop at the corner of Mechanic Street, watched the brake lights glow and the taunting rhythms of her turn signal.

I wiped up the milk that had coated the breakfast table and dripped onto the kitchen floor. I did the dishes and then I went upstairs. I brushed my teeth and got into the unmade bed. I closed my eyes, and lay there a few minutes. I could smell Gloria on the sheets, her night cream and a trace of that musty smell of sleep I'd dreamed of coming home to.

I wondered how often she used to go back to bed after I'd left for the office and she'd gotten Mark and Tobin off to school. I wondered if I'm even capable of sleeping at night anymore. I don't think so. Friday and Saturday nights I watch TV or go to the drive-in and then come home and read till morning. Sometimes I go down to Brainard Lake and fish all night. I can see the lights of the town all laid out, and I sit there in my boat on the dark water watching them, the way angels watch over people's lives in old movies. Some nights, on weekends, I tiptoe into Gloria's room and watch her sleeping. I sit and watch her by the light from the street, her heavy breathing, the slackness of her mouth, the way her cheeks are drawn in. She looks older and more careworn, not the way I think of her nights when I'm alone at work.

I GOT UP, PULLED ON my jeans and my rumpled Pinkerton shirt and went into my study. I don't do much reading here in the mornings. I mostly just sit and enjoy the space. The Navaho chief's blanket on the floor has a diamond pattern, and it keeps a diamond pattern no matter how many times you fold it. I showed Mark its secret the last time he was home. "Neat, Dad," he said, "that's really neat." Mark would never tell me himself, he's too polite for that, but I could see the disappointment in his eyes. He'd molded himself after me, and now I'm not what I was anymore. Mark lives in Hong Kong. He works for Eastman Kodak. He's the youngest executive in their international division. He flies to Thailand and Malaysia, all the places Conrad wrote about, but for him it's like going to Chicago. "You wouldn't believe the buys you can get," he tells me. He bought me a custom-made suit I've never worn and a Sony tape recorder no bigger than a cigarette pack.

I love Mark. I wish we could be closer. I don't mean his living so far away; I wish I could feel about him the way I feel about Tobin. Mark is everything I could've wanted him to be, practical, ambitious. He's caring and still a little bit ruthless. He's more me than I was, I suppose, but he's not like Tobin. I learned from Tobin things I never could've taught him. But there aren't many people like Tobin. From the time he was a baby, you could see it in his eyes. He knew something. I could tell him things I couldn't tell anybody else, things I've dreamed, things that scare me sometimes, things that if I told Gloria, she'd just look at me with that look of hers, that look that says, "Who is this man? Did I marry this man?"

I told him my dream about the princess, how I was standing in the crowd, looking up at the scaffold, how they would bring her out and how there was this banquet table just below, spread with every good thing in the world you could imagine. I told him how I wanted to rescue her, but that I was trapped in the crowd below, watching, and I couldn't move, and how, each time, just as they got ready to bring down the axe, she would get up and come down from the scaffold, down to the banquet table, and have another piece of cake. And Tobin smiled at me, and he said, "I love that dream, Dad. I think I know the princess, the one who refuses to die."

I don't know what would've happened if he'd lived. I think

maybe he wasn't hard enough for this world. I think that when he died, something in me died too, that something Tobin didn't have that had gotten me so far up the ladder at Clark's. But I just didn't care anymore. There were other things, private things. I didn't want to see my friends. Their sympathy felt like an accusation. "It's not your fault!" they said. But why did they say it? They tried to cheer me up. I put in my time for a while, but when I saw how that was hurting the company, I resigned. Everybody wanted to help. Jay Campbell told me that any time I wanted to talk he wanted to listen.

SOMETIMES I JUST SIT and look at the poster of Van Gogh's bedroom and admire the simplicity of it, the way it describes his life: the bed, the pitcher and bowl, the two rush chairs, a few pictures on the wall and one book on the table. I wonder what the book is. Dickens probably. He loved Dickens. How rough the floor looks, as if it needed sanding. You can almost feel the splinters under your feet. The window in the painting is open just a crack, and as I look at it I feel as if I'm about to get up and walk across the room and open it wide and see the fields of wheat and bright flowers or to look down on the town square of Arles and see Roulin, the postman, coming this way with a letter from Tobin. I open that window again and again, and it's never the Eckerts' immaculate patio.

I HAVE TO GET SOME SLEEP now. I have to get up in time to start dinner before Gloria comes home. It's usually just something frozen or some pasta with canned sauce. Some nights she eats downtown. I go down to the kitchen and get a couple of beers from the fridge. I come back up to my room, put my feet on the window ledge and lean back in my chair. There's a breeze moving through the maple leaves, and if I close my eyes, I can imagine it's the sound of a stream. In the book I was reading last night, the general died by a stream in the mountains. His army had been destroyed in an ambush by Victoriano Huerta in Chihuahua, and the general had been pursued into the mountains, where he died of his wounds. As a young child in Oaxaca he had lived by a stream. He was still a young man, and he had lost everything. The love of the American woman was only a memory as he dragged his torn body through the rocks and sage. But he had a moment of happiness before he died. He had that small victory, just making it to the stream and laying his head down by the cool rushing of its water.

HOMECOMING

There was no reason for me to suspect my father had ever been unfaithful to my mother, but the second day I was home, she confronted me with the possibility. I was unloading the washing machine when she came into the utility room. She closed the door behind her, isolating us from my Uncle Audley and her sisters, Ellen and Arlene, who had come to stay with her until after the funeral, and turned to me with the question that had obviously been haunting her from the moment she knew he was dead.

"David, your father was a fine man," she began, "but . . ." She turned to watch the snow swirling in the alcove that separated us from the rest of the house. "But he wasn't perfect, you know."

"Nobody is, Mom." I couldn't imagine what was coming.

"Well, I wonder . . . no, it's not just that. I just know. I just feel certain your father was seeing someone."

"Seeing someone? You mean like a shrink?"

"No, I don't mean a shrink. I mean another woman."

"You think so? You think Dad had a girlfriend?"

"There's this book of love poems." She had been holding a small leather-bound volume. I had assumed it was an address book. "This book is three-quarters full of love poems, in your

165

father's own hand." She held the book open like a prosecutor displaying evidence to a jury.

"Dad wrote love poems?"

"Shakespeare, Browning. He copied them down, word for word, but who for? He never showed them to me."

"Maybe he meant them for you," I suggested. "Maybe he just liked love poems."

"Oh, David!" She flung the book into a basket half full of clean clothes, held her arms out, and stumbled across the room to embrace me. "I don't know what I think. He seemed so distant. He seemed to be off somewhere else in his thoughts these last few years. I couldn't bear it if I thought there was another woman he loved." She was sniffling, and I could feel her head wagging against my shoulder.

"Then don't think it," I said.

"But what if it's true?"

"Look, Mom, he's gone." I put my hands on her shoulders and held her at arm's length so that I could look her in the eye. "You're not going to lose him to any other woman, so what's the difference? Why even think about it? Why torment yourself?"

"But if he died thinking of her . . . ?"

"Mom, stop it! You lived together forty-some years . . ."

"Thirty-eight," she corrected me.

"Okay, thirty-eight. That's what's important. I don't think there ever was anyone but you, and if there was, it doesn't matter now."

SOMEHOW I'D THOUGHT it would be different, that I would come home to her and we would comfort each other and find ourselves brought close, at least for a little while. I felt my temples throbbing and a heaviness in my chest as if all the oxygen had been sucked out of the room. I left her there, quietly weeping, and walked out through the living room where Uncle Audley and my aunts were going over the funeral arrangements. I avoided looking at them, picked my jacket up off the chair by the door and stepped out onto the porch. The cold wind and the snow on my face felt as welcome as the first breath after a long swim underwater. I headed down Elm Street, stepping gingerly from footprint to footprint on the unshoveled sidewalk, trying, as best I could, to keep the snow out of my shoes. At the corner, I turned right, toward Main.

I hoped my father had had an affair. I hoped some woman had taken him over and made him forget about everything else, but knowing my father, I doubted it. He'd lived his life as a truly good man. He had been the loan officer at the bank and had made too many farm loans that went bad. He believed that if a man was sincere and did his best, it would see him through, but in farming, all too frequently, sincerity wasn't enough. He tried real estate at a time when everyone was trying real estate and home mortgage rates had gone to sixteen percent. He tried insurance and, because he was so well liked and widely trusted, he did well at it, though he had confided in me that at times it made him feel like a confidence man. "It's getting people to bet against themselves," he told me one cold morning in a duck blind, just before I was to leave for New York. "Sometimes I feel as though I should be wearing a green eyeshade, like a blackjack dealer."

I suppose it was largely because of his dissatisfaction with the way things had turned out for him that my father had encouraged me to go to New York. Gary Haily and the Microbes had heard my tapes and made me an offer. It wasn't much money to start with, but they had gigs lined up and a contract for a record with CBS. I'd started saxophone lessons in the fifth grade, won a music scholarship to Michigan and played with a group in college. My mother had begged me to take the job I'd been offered as Band Director at Brainard Junior High, but when the offer came from New York, my father said, "Take it." He called me down to his office to talk about it. "Don't tell your mother I told you this, but if you don't try it, you'll always wonder what might have happened. You're good. Get out of this town. Be somebody."

I think in his later years my success in music was about the only thing that brought my father any joy, that and hunting, unless of course my mother's suspicions about another woman were justified. A few minutes after I'd gotten home, she asked me to get rid of his guns. "I just want them out of here," she said. "I don't care what you do with them." I called Glen Hopkins who had run Hopkins Sporting Goods for as long as I could remember and discovered that Glen had died five years earlier. I made arrangements with his son, Mike, to drop the guns off for appraisal and sale on consignment. Then she asked me to dispose of his clothes. "I can't look at them and think about their never being worn again," she said. I went through his closets, packed up his belongings and took them to Goodwill, all but his grey fedora, his field compass and his Masonic ring, which I decided to keep. Within twenty-four hours I had moved almost every trace of my father out of the house. It seemed a little abrupt, but it was her house now, and it was what she wanted.

My father had always wanted to travel, to see Java and Bali and Kuala Lumpur because they were the most foreign-sounding places he could imagine, but he never got out of the U.S. except for a few long weekends in Canada. He came to see me in New York once. The band was rehearsing for a tour so I only had a few hours a day to spend with him. I'd drop him off at the Met or the Museum of Natural History, and when I'd pick him up in the evening, he would describe, with an almost evangelical enthusiasm, everything he had seen. My mother never liked to travel. It was too disrupting, she said, and she had too many community responsibilities. If she wasn't at a bridge party, a planning commission or a United Way meeting, she was home on the phone. I think she felt she had to make contact with everyone she knew at least once a day out of a fear she might be forgotten.

My father was up at his cabin north of White Cloud when he died. Henry Klomp and Jerry Eshler had gone up to join him for some rabbit hunting on Sunday morning, and they found him on the floor in front of the fireplace. The fire had gone cold and so had he. It was apparent from the coroner's report that he'd had a heart attack early Saturday evening and died some-time toward morning. I wondered what or who he had thought about as he lay dying. "Life and death are like poles on a mag-net," he'd told me when my dog Skipper died. "You can try to cut one off, but no matter how many times you cut it, you're still going to have them both."

ON MAIN STREET IT STRUCK ME how things had changed in the decade I'd been away. The street looked like a movie set. I had never realized before how low the buildings were, one or two stories except for Brainard Home Furnishings which rose three. There weren't many people on the street, and those that were out walked hunched up against the cold. I pulled the collar of my jacket up around my ears and felt a tightening in my neck and shoulders. I pushed my hands deeper into the pockets and felt the cool sharp edges of the key to my father's office. I'd promised my mother I would go through his desk and sort out any personal papers. I wondered just how personal the papers might be and if there might be things best kept from her. The clock on the bank flashed a minus 7 degrees Celsius, then 20 Fahrenheit and then the time, 4:25. I passed Curley's Dime Store. There was plywood where the plate glass had been, and the "U" and the "Y" were missing from the gilded sign above the door. I looked across the street into Ed's Barber Shop, and saw a stranger in a barber's tunic sitting in the chair by the window, reading the paper. I remembered, as a child, frequently waiting over an hour for my turn in the chair, learning important lessons about fishing, politics and women on my way to a fresh crewcut. I felt the key again and realized I'd been tumbling it in my fingers like a lucky coin. I started across the street and then saw the red neon sign above the bar, two doors down.

The smell of Bob's Bar was one thing that hadn't changed, a warm dispiriting mixture of beer, cigarette smoke, urinal wafers and cow manure. Even coming in from the late afternoon dark of the street, it took a few minutes for my eyes to adjust to the gloom. There were two men sitting at the bar, and I could tell, by the sour milk taint of their coveralls, they were farmers. They talked in low voices, left off their conversation for a moment and made a half turn to check me out as I took a stool just down from them.

"I coulda told him that kid wouldn't last six weeks," the one closest to me continued, "but he didn't ask me, so I figured, hell, let him find out for himself."

Having been away for so long, it was like entering a strange bar, and I felt a little tentative until I heard the growl of Mick's voice. "Well, jump start my heart! Davey Townsend, is that you?"

There was no mistaking Micky Street, at 400 pounds, literally the biggest man in the county and the reason Bob's had maintained the reputation of being a fairly orderly place. He reached across the bar and shook me playfully by the shoulder. "I thought maybe you'd forgot about us now you're famous."

"I'm not famous, Mick."

He set a bottle of Stroh's down in front of me and then turned to the two farmers down the bar. "Hey Gene, Clare, this here's Davey Townsend. He's a famous musician."

"Come on, Mick!" I pleaded. I hadn't expected this.

"Oh sure." The one closest to us swung around on his stool. "You had Santa Claus in here a couple of weeks ago."

"No really. This guy shot pool in here from the time he was that high. He's been on national TV. He's made records. You can buy 'em over at Musicland."

"No kidding?" The farmers both got up off their stools. One of them was chewing on a toothpick. "Got to get back for chores, Mick."

"You Bill Townsend's boy?" the taller one asked. There was a two-day stubble on his face, and his eyes had a kind of sad rheumy look.

I nodded.

"Sorry about your dad," he said. "He was a fine fella. Not many like him anymore. Sorry he's gone."

"Thank you," I said. "I'm sorry too."

"You gonna take over for him?" the shorter one stopped on his way out.

"Take over?"

"Up the street." He nodded in my direction. "The insurance."

"No. I live in New York," I said.

"In New York City?"

"Yup."

"Right in the city?"

"Yup," I said again.

"Too bad." He pulled the toothpick from his lips and made a loud sucking noise. "Not many like your dad. Pretty hard to fill his shoes." He followed his friend out, and a little swirl of snow blew in as the door closed behind them.

"I'm sorry too, Davey," Mick said. "I meant to say that. Your dad come in here once in a while. He talked about you a lot. Don't pay attention to those guys." He gestured toward the door with his thumb.

"Was he happy, Mick, do you think?"

"What's happy?" Mick stopped wiping the bar and flung the towel over his shoulder. "Compared to what I see mostly, he was happy. I don't know if he had a lot of fun, but he cared about people, and a lot of people cared about him."

"I hope he had some fun," I said.

"Hey, listen to this," Mick said. He turned and lumbered down to the end of the bar and crossed the room to the jukebox. I felt another cold draft as the door opened again. A woman came in. She hesitated and then walked over and took a seat on the stool next to mine. Mick punched several buttons on the jukebox. By the time he got back behind the bar, "Arriba," the Microbes' first hit, was playing. "How about that, huh? We got all your singles in that machine."

"That's nice, Mick," I smiled. "I can't think of anywhere I'd rather have 'em."

"Black Jack and water?" Mick called to the woman.

"Please, Mick."

I turned to look at her, and she didn't seem like the type for Bob's. She was wearing a long grey cloth coat and black knee boots. Mick set the drink down in front of her. "Davey, this is Barbara."

"How are you?" I turned toward her.

"Hello," she said. She bowed her head slightly and looked me in the eyes as she spoke. "You're David Townsend, aren't you?"

"Yes, I am. How did you know?"

Mick was washing glasses at the other end of the bar. "Hey, I like this part, Davey," he hollered as the record came to my saxophone break.

"I remember you from school," the woman said.

173

I was trying to ignore the record and Mick's groans of pleasure accompanying my solo. "What's your last name? Or what was it?"

"Ruhl. Barbara Ruhl. Still is. I don't think you'd remember me."

I studied her face. There was something familiar about it, but I didn't really remember her. If I hadn't been looking into her eyes, it was a face I probably wouldn't have looked at twice. It was a little too thin, the chin a little too weak, but her eyes were quite direct, and she had beautiful hair that hung to her shoulders. Dark brown, I thought. I couldn't be sure in the dim light of the bar.

"No, I don't," I admitted, "I'm not very good at names and faces. Were you in my class?"

"No, I was four or five years ahead of you. That's one reason you wouldn't remember. But I remember your saxophone playing and . . ." She hesitated. "And I saw you from my window just a few minutes ago. I saw you come in here, and I knew it was you."

"Really? After all these years?" It seemed remarkable that an older girl would remember me from school. "Did you recognize me from a photograph on an album?"

"A photograph, yes. But not from an album."

"Hey Davey!" Mick hollered. "Can I play that one again?"

"Not that one, Mick. Play something else."

"How about 'Snow Lily'?"

"No, Mick. I'm tired of the Microbes. How about Bruce Springsteen or the Police?"

"We ain't got any Police."

"Anything's okay, Mick."

"Take your chances," he said.

"You said you saw me from your window." I turned back to Barbara Ruhl, and she was smiling over my exchange with Mick. "Do you live on Main Street, upstairs?"

"No, my office window."

"Where do you work?"

"Just down the street. I worked for your father."

I stared at her for a moment. "That's where you saw the photograph?"

"On his desk." She nodded.

"That's funny, because I was actually heading for my dad's office when I changed my mind and came here."

"I know." She put her hand on my arm. "Your mother called and told me to tell you when you came in that you're supposed to be at the funeral home at 7:00."

"We'll pretend I didn't come in."

"Well you didn't, actually."

"That's right. I'm glad you're keeping me honest." I raised my beer in a toast to her, and as I did, something clicked for me. The hair had been different, curled around her face in a pageboy, and there was an oversized cardigan sweater with a big blue "B" on it, a straight skirt to midcalf, bobby sox and saddle shoes, a vision as clear as it had been when I was twelve.

"Artie Bentenhausen," I said.

"What?"

"I remember you now. You used to go with Artie Bentenhausen, the best basketball player Brainard High ever had. You used to wear his letter sweater."

"Oh my gosh!" She laughed and covered her mouth. "You remember that?"

"I used to fantasize about you when I'd see you in school. I used to dream that I was Artie."

"Not really?"

"And you were Homecoming queen too, weren't you?"

"No, but I was on the court."

"Well, you should have been queen, I thought."

"I can't believe that. Now it's kind of just the other way around."

"How do you mean?"

"Well, now you're the star, and Artie's working down at the Co-op. Now I'm the one who dreams about you."

"You dream about me?"

"Well, almost. I've followed your career. I heard so much about you from your dad. You were almost like some mythical being. You never came back to Brainard, and I couldn't relate you to the little kid with the saxophone in the school band."

I had two more beers and Barbara had another Jack Daniels. She told me how she and Artie had gotten married after high school, and then divorced three years later, how she was glad she hadn't been able to get pregnant, and had just wanted to pretend the marriage never happened. I told her I hadn't had time for marriage, how most of the women I met came on to me because I was a rock star, and that if there was one I cared about, being on the road more than half the year made anything lasting almost impossible.

"I'm not complaining," I said. "It's the life I chose, but it gets old."

"What else would you ever do?" she asked.

"I don't know. I come back home and everyone wants to know if I'm going to start selling insurance."

"It's funny how we look at other people's lives," she said. "You wanted to be Artie, and now thousands of kids want to be you, or like what they think you are." She glanced at the Stroh's Beer clock behind the bar. "I hate to break this up," she put her hand on my arm again, "but it is almost seven."

"I don't really feel like going," I said. "Can I see you later?"

She gave me her address, upstairs in the back, on a street just three blocks from where I'd grown up. I tried to pay for our drinks, but Mick wouldn't take anything, and I left for the funeral home.

I REMEMBERED RANDY BINGHAM, the mortician, who greeted me at the door, and I remembered most of the faces and some of the names of the people who told me how nice it was to see me back home and how they were sorry it had to be under these circumstances. My father's body was on display in an open casket, not my father but an effigy, like a bad painting done from memory. I turned away after the first glance and didn't look again. "Your dad thought the world of you," Henry Klomp said. "You were the bright spot in his life." And then he added, "You and your mom, of course."

My mother held up pretty well, in fact I was amazed at how strong she seemed. She was happy to have her brother, my Uncle Audley, there with her, and she seemed to be more of a comfort to the people who came through the reception line than they were to her. I was introduced to the members of her bridge club, her golf league, the Ladies Hospital Auxiliary and her garden club. My father's garden had been a big plot of zinnias. I remember how on summer evenings he would sit on the back steps and admire them. All he grew was zinnias, and he loved them because they grew in so many different colors, and they took so little care. In late summer and early fall, he would take a bouquet of zinnias to every client he called on. I thought it would have been appropriate if there had been zinnias at the funeral home, but of course there weren't any.

Barbara came through the line, and we shook hands. She hugged my mother and told her not to worry about anything at the agency.

"Oh thank you, Barbara," my mother said. "You were so much help to Bill. He told me he couldn't have managed without you."

The gathering dwindled to those few friends and relatives who would be going back to the house with my mother. "I have a little more work to do at the office," I told her, and she hugged me gratefully.

"You sound just like your father," she said. She gave me a fierce smile and blotted a tear from the corner of her eye.

THE WIND HAD DIED DOWN. The sky had cleared, and the stars were brilliant in the dark rivers above the lighted streets. The snow creaked under my feet, and I picked out the Pleiades, Orion and a few other constellations my father had taught me when we'd been on camping trips, hunting or fishing in the Upper Peninsula. When I turned the corner at Mechanic, I could see the nearly full moon just coming over the trees.

Barbara's apartment was small but comfortable, with the slightly stuffy gas stove smell I remembered from the houses of friends when I was a child. Among the pictures on her sitting room wall were several of my father, including one with me, taken after I'd won a first division in the state instrumental music finals. She'd picked up a six-pack of the beer I'd been drinking at Bob's. She poured herself another Jack Daniels, and we sat at her kitchen table and talked about people we remembered from school and what had become of them. One of her classmates had become head of the Drug Enforcement Administration in Washington, she told me. Her best friend in high school had moved to Australia with her husband and wrote to her every year at Christmas to tell her about their sheep ranch and how she hoped someday she would come visit them. "And you, of course," she said. "You're the one who gets talked about the most. I'm sure your life can't measure up to the stories, but you're Brainard's famous person. Your father talked about you almost every day. He'd say things like, 'The new record is number twenty-five with a bullet. How about that?'" She held her hand over her mouth, in my father's characteristic gesture, and then swung it away with the palm upturned. "He picked up all that kind of music talk. I'd come in in the morning, and first thing, he'd look at his calendar and tell me, 'David's playing Cambridge tonight. That's in Massachusetts.'" She mimicked his mouth wave again. "'That's where Harvard College is, you know.'"

At first it was just tears, and then her mouth pulled at the edges so that she could hardly finish her sentence. I reached over and took her hand. "Hey, what is it?" I asked.

179

"Your dad. Oh please," she said, "hold me."

I took her in my arms. I could smell the perfume of her hair, and I could feel her body trembling with suppressed sobs. Barbara Ruhl, I said to myself. I thought of her in Artie Bentenhausen's letter sweater and thought how odd it seemed to be holding her in my arms now. "I know," I said. "I know."

"Can you stay here for a while?" she asked. We were both feeling empty, and it seemed as natural as taking her in my arms when she'd begun to cry.

"I want to," I said. She got up and led me into the bedroom. We didn't make love, though I wanted to. I felt closer to her than to any woman I'd met in years. We lay on her quilted bedspread, fully clothed, and held each other close for a long time.

The moon shone in through the window so that I could see her quite clearly. I felt completely relaxed. I felt as if the past ten years had been a dream. I looked out the window at the moonlight on the snow and the shadows of the few big maples in the yard and wondered how long it had been since I'd slept in someone's house, a house on a street with trees in the yard and not a hotel or a condominium or a bus or a plane.

She held my head to her shoulder, and then she kissed me on the ear and whispered, "Thank you."

"You don't have to thank me," I laughed.

"I feel better now," she said.

I stifled a yawn and stretched against the headboard. "You know what I've missed?" I said.

"No. What have you missed?"

"Driving around in the country, looking at barns."

"Looking at barns?"

"I'm always on my way somewhere, the next concert, the next set of faces in the next town. I thought about that on my way over from the funeral home. I walked past houses and saw the lights inside and realized that all the time I've been gone, those people have been living there, and how little things have probably changed for them, how they might live all their lives there, perfectly happy."

"Have you ever thought about moving back?"

"No, not seriously. I mean, what would I do?"

"Drive around and look at barns, I guess." She smiled, and I held her close and thought how I wanted to keep that moment, the moon shining through the window, the furnace blower whirring, the smell of her hair, the feel of her breath on my neck.

"How did you come to work for my dad?" I asked.

"I met him in Indianapolis."

"Why in Indianapolis?" I backed away on the pillow and looked at her.

"Oh, I knew who he was, of course, but I don't think I'd ever talked to him. I was working for the Frome Agency, and I'd become the top secretary. Mr. Frome wanted me to start taking over some accounts and doing some claims work. He was all set to go down to Indianapolis for our company's annual sales convention when he got the flu, so he sent me down in his place. And I felt really lost there. I think your father saw that. I know he did, because he told me later. I was in the ballroom of the hotel where the convention was, not knowing anyone or who I should talk to or where I should be looking or what I should be doing with my hands. I had three or four drinks, more than I was used to, and your father came over and introduced himself and said he'd like to take me out to dinner if he could, and I thanked him. I could see right through him, and I laughed out loud, I was so relieved to have someone to talk to. I told him I was afraid I just didn't belong there in that room full of important people, and he said, Oh, you belong all right, maybe not here, but that the people who really did belong there probably didn't belong anywhere else. We went to a restaurant on the top of the tallest building in Indianapolis and had duck with orange sauce and oysters and champagne, and I thought your father was the kindest man I'd ever met."

I watched her eyes as she told me their story, and I knew that she had loved him and had probably told him so, and I thought how I never had. It was something men didn't say to each other. It might be understood, but you didn't say it. I'd been on the verge of telling him the last time we'd talked on the phone, about a month before he died, but something stopped me. I thought it would seem silly, like telling a blind man about a beautiful sunset. I don't know. What could he have said? I love you too? And where would we have gone from there?

So this is the other woman, I thought. For a moment I thought about asking her, but then decided it would have spoiled things, would have been too obvious, like telling my father I loved him, and she would have been embarrassed or offended.

"When do you have to go back?" she asked.

"Tomorrow, right after the service. I've got a flight out tomorrow evening. I left the band in the middle of a tour, and I've got to be in Atlanta on Thursday."

"Won't your mother need you?"

"I don't think she will. I've done about all I can for her. My Uncle Audley's going to stay for a couple of weeks at least, and she's really closer to him. What about you?" I asked. "What are you going to do now?"

"Stay on and run the agency, if your mother wants me to. I learned the ropes pretty well from your dad."

IT WAS ABOUT 2:00 A.M. when I left Barbara's apartment. She put her arms around my neck and kissed me good-bye at the door. "Thank you, David," she said again. "You've helped to keep your dad alive for me."

"Yeah," I nodded, "me too."

"And don't worry about his papers. I've got everything in order for your mother."

"Oh my God," I said. "I never did get to his office."

"No," she smiled, "but I won't tell. I guess I won't be seeing you again, other than the funeral, I mean."

"No, I guess not," I said. I kissed her one more time and then walked down the stairs. The packed snow was slippery under my shoes, and I held onto the railing for support. I stopped at the corner of her block and watched her window until the light went out, and then I walked home, and all the houses were dark.

MY MOTHER PUT ON A BRAVE face for the funeral, and at the house after the service she expressed her gratitude to everyone for coming and for the friendship and kindness they'd shown

Dad. "If he could see you here today, he'd know just what a great success his life really was. Thank you all," she concluded.

I'd never seen that kind of nobility in my mother before. Maybe losing Dad had brought it out in her. Maybe it was there all along and I couldn't see it. If she still had any anxiety about there having been another woman in his life, she kept it hidden, and I noticed that the little leather-bound volume of love poems had been retrieved from the laundry basket and lay prominently on the desk in the living room. She hugged me as I left the house, and I promised I'd call in a couple of days.

Uncle Audley drove me down to Grand Rapids, to the airport, and he talked about how Mother had a lot of friends, and how, now that he'd retired from International Harvester, he and Aunt Lydia had been thinking of moving to Brainard.

"I'll be able to send her some money if she needs it," I told him.

"I know you will," Uncle Audley said, "but your dad had a lot of insurance."

It was just getting dark as we got to the airport, and it had started snowing again. Big flakes settled on my shoulders and my sleeves as I got my bag out of the trunk. I shook hands with Uncle Audley, and I stood there and watched him drive away. I had about an hour before my flight left. I had a beer, and I bought a *Time* and the new *Rolling Stone*. I thought about Barbara at the funeral and how she'd seemed to be having such a difficult time. I thought about her telling me of her first meeting with my father, and I wanted to talk with her once more. I didn't have her phone number, but it was only 5:30. I figured she might still be at the office. I called and had just barely given the operator my credit card number when the ringing stopped. I could feel my heart pounding, and I waited a second to hear her say hello. But there was a click, and then I heard my father's voice. "Hi. This is Bill Townsend. No one's here right now, but if you'll leave a message after the beep, I'll get back to you as soon as I can. Thanks for calling. You have thirty seconds to leave your message."

I choked and started coughing, but got control of it just after the beep came along. I listened, a little bit stunned, to the faint hum of the recorder running on, and then I suddenly felt very happy.

About the Author

Dan Gerber's poems and stories have been published in a variety of magazines and anthologies, including *The Nation, The New Yorker, Poetry, The Georgia Review, Playboy, Sports Illustrated,* and *The Best American Poetry 1999.* His most recent novel is *A Voice from the River,* and his two most recent collections of poems are *A Last Bridge Home: New and Selected Poems* and *Trying to Catch the Horses.* He divides his time between the Santa Inez Valley in California and the Idaho-Wyoming border.

DESIGNED AND COMPOSED IN ADOBE CASLON BY

WILSTED & TAYLOR PUBLISHING SERVICES,

OAKLAND, CALIFORNIA

PRINTED AND BOUND BY

THOMSON-SHORE, INC.,

DEXTER, MICHIGAN